SPUR #2

CATHOUSE KITTEN

DIRK FLETCHER

LEISURE BOOKS  NEW YORK CITY

A LEISURE BOOK®

June 2003

Published by

Dorchester Publishing Co., Inc.
276 Fifth Avenue
New York, NY 10001

ISBN 0-8439-2078-5

Printed in the United States of America.

CHAPTER 1

AUGUST, 1869—NEAR ABILENE, KANSAS.

(Andrew Johnson had been succeeded as President of the United States by Ulysses S. Grant. Secretary of State William H. Seward was still the butt of jokes for paying more than seven million dollars to buy "worthless" Alaska from Russia the year before. It was known as "Seward's Folly." The Civil War had ended four years earlier but antagonism between North and South still ran high. The United Secret Service was established by an act of Congress in 1865 with William P. Wood as its first director. The telegraph was completed coast to coast in 1861. Work on the transcontinental railroad was finished in Promontory, Utah. Now the great new nation was truly linked from East to West.)

It was only a card game, a harmless way to pass the time on the long train ride from St. Louis west on the Eastern Division of the Union Pacific Railroad. Penny poker, no raise over a nickel, so no one could lose much. The game had lasted four hours and it was now midafternoon. Two players slid back their chairs and left the small table. The club car was thick with smoke when "new money" sat down in an empty spot opposite Spur McCoy.

He looked up, squinting through his own cigar smoke that drifted back into his eyes. What he saw made him stub out the stogie and jump to his feet.

"Miss! Excuse me—I didn't realize you were there. I mean, I didn't know you were a woman—I mean. . . . My apologies!"

She was gorgeous, with summer-wheat blonde hair worn loose around her shoulders and cut in straight bangs over soft green eyes. She was a foot shorter than Spur, neatly dressed, and what he could see of her figure was interesting. Her short brown jacket was open at the front, revealing a white blouse that buttoned to her chin but stretched delightfully over full breasts. Her traveling skirt of matching brown swept the floor.

She smiled up at him. Her face was pert and pretty, with a freckled nose and delicious red lips that wore more than a hint of rouge.

"Your apology is accepted, sir," she said and lifted artfully arched brows. "Good Lord! I do hope the man's knees work. It's going to be awkward playing poker if he must stand the whole time."

Spur laughed, a deep, warm baritone, as he dropped back into his chair. He had on his "working clothes" for this assignment: a brown business suit, white shirt with a brown high stiff white collar, a yellow checkered vest, brown tie and boots vanishing under brown trousers.

He glanced at the other man at the table, a short, rotund drummer from St. Louis. "I believe we have a new player. I hope you don't mind."

The salesman snorted, stood and pocketed the stack of pennies, dimes and nickels in front of him. He touched a sweaty brow.

"I don't mind, but our company rule is never play poker with no woman." He looked at her quickly. "No offense, ma'am." He stepped away, a wave of body odor following him down the club car.

"It's 'Miss'," she said, "and no offense taken." The woman looked back at Spur. "Now, are we going to play cards or not?"

Spur grinned and his lips parted, showing even, white teeth. "The railroad management has been warning us about card sharks on board. Do you carry your own deck?"

She laughed and he liked the sound. "No, I'm afraid not. I'm on my way to Abilene, and since you're the most attractive man on the train, I decided to meet you." She held out her hand. "I'm Abby Newland from Chicago."

Spur took her fingers gently. He caught a brief scent of her perfume, a light fragrance of wildflowers.

"Miss Newland, I am most pleased to meet you. I'm Spur McCoy and I'm from St. Louis." He let go of her hand reluctantly, and was interested to note the way she met his stare with one as frank, appreciative, and evaluating as his own. That was most unusual behavior for a woman here or in the East.

"Poker—well, we can play if you'd like. But we're only about an hour out of Abilene. Perhaps we could sit and talk instead?" The train gave a long whistle and gritty coal smoke blew past the window in a black fog.

She nodded. They moved to the window seats and watched the flat lands of Kansas roll by as they talked. Spur relaxed and enjoyed himself. Banter with a pretty woman was always recreation for him. For the moment he forgot his assignment, he forgot the fact that he was a United States Secret Service agent going to Abilene on a dangerous job.

The girl was young, beautiful, and fascinating. He could think of a few more enjoyable ways to while away the last hours of a trip. General Halleck in Washington, D.C. wouldn't deny him one moment of relaxation. Spur often thought the general forgot about the assignments he handed out the second after doing so. Spur looked back at the delightful girl and couldn't help but smile.

By the time the train pulled into Abilene, he had learned that she was coming to town to make plans for opening a Harvey House depot restaurant that would serve good food that rail travelers could enjoy. It was a whole new idea for Kansas. Instead of quick snacks, there would be real restaurant-quality food, served with class and dignity, not the usual ten minute stop by the train for a hash-house "bite and run."

She seemed fascinated by his name.

"I've never known anyone called Spur. Did you get the name because you do a lot of riding and wear spurs? Are you a real cowboy?"

"I ride, but I'm not a real cowboy. The work is too

hard and dangerous and dirty. Besides, I hate cows. Did I tell you I'm stopping at Abilene, too?"

Her face brightened. She reached out and touched his hand in a small gesture of familiarity that surprised him. "I'm so glad that . . ." She looked down as if trying to decide whether or not to continue, then plunged ahead. "Would you think me brazen if I suggested that I would just love to go out for dinner tonight if I could find anyone to invite me? It's been such a tiring trip that the two things I want most are a good hot bath and a fine dinner."

"I don't think that would be brazen at all. And I'd be delighted to escort you. Just remember, this isn't Chicago. Abilene is a rough, rugged, brand new little cattle town. It wasn't even here a year and a half ago. Joseph Geiting McCoy came in and made a town out of a railroad way-station. But he did put up the Drover's Cottage hotel, and the dining room is one of the best out here in the plains. No, he's no relation of mine. But I will be staying at the Drover's Cottage."

She laughed and he marveled at the way her green eyes lighted up. "Now that is a strange coincidence! That's where I'm staying. We might just bump into each other."

"Sounds possible." Spur moved his hand so it touched hers and a sudden warm feeling surged through him.

"Miss Newland, would you allow me to help you with your luggage and to get you settled in the hotel?"

"Mr. McCoy! What a nice, neighborly thing to do. I would appreciate it so much, I feel like a stranger in a strange land."

A half hour later the train arrived in Abilene on a hot, sticky August afternoon. They moved their bags to the hotel and when they registered, discovered that their rooms were next to each other. He stood inside near the door and was glad that the heavy, hot Kansas air was not quite so warm here. She sat down on the bed and bounced twice.

"Good—just right, not too soft." Abby Newland stood and stretched like a young cougar, then took off the short brown jacket she wore for traveling. She took a deep breath and Spur marveled at what that did to the demure white blouse. Abby walked over to him with a slight sway of her hips.

"I haven't thanked you for helping me get settled and all."

She was so much shorter than Spur that she had to reach up and pull his face down to her eager lips. She kissed him seriously, her slender body pressed tightly against his. When Abby broke off the kiss she clung to him. Her perfume intoxicated Spur.

"Have I shocked you, Spur McCoy?" she asked coquettishly.

He looked down at the beautiful, sexy girl in his arms and smiled. "Not at all, Abby. In fact, I had something like this in mind, myself." His hand found one of her breasts and he caressed it softly.

She smiled. "My goodness, you are so *slow!*"

"Not too slow, I hope," he said and kissed her, his tongue thrusting into her open mouth. His hand closed fully over her breast and pressed it more insistently. Abby moaned. When the kiss ended, she opened the top buttons of her blouse, watching him all the while. Then she quickly unbuttoned the rest and pulled off the blouse. She seemed to be seeking his approval as she slid out of the brief chemise, and stood before him, bare to the waist.

"Beautiful!" Spur said. She was. Her full breasts had erect pink nipples the size of thimbles, surrounded by areolas of a deeper rose color

"Marvelous, magnificent!" Spur said, breathing faster.

"Kiss them," she said. "I've waited all day long for you to look at me, to touch me, to kiss me."

Spur laughed softly, picked her up in one swoop and carried her to the bed where he dropped her. Abby squealed as she bounced on the mattress, then sat up and patted the bed beside her.

"You are so tall and handsome, Spur McCoy. I can't resist red-haired men. And your moustache tickles when we kiss!" She leaned back seductively against the pillows, looking up at him through thick, golden lashes.

Spur sat beside her, his body responding, surging, wanting her. But something told him to hold back—this was all too easy. Something was off key, out of place. Why was she doing this? She was much too young and beautiful to have to throw herself at any man. What was the snare?

Her tongue toyed with his ear, licking around the edge, darting inside, driving him crazy. She moved closer, her soft breasts crushed against his side, his chest. He watched silently as she opened his vest, then his shirt and her fingers caressed the curling hair. Then she caught his head with both hands and pulled him down toward her delicious breasts.

Spur gave a little sigh of surrender, bent and savored the closest pink morsel, so silky smooth, yet vibrant and pulsating with her sudden desire that made her whole body tremble.

Slowly, deliberately he anointed each swaying half globe, kissing the nipples, then nibbling on them, bringing pleased gasps from Abby. Her hands caught his and slid them down to her waist where he unbuttoned fasteners and pushed down her long skirt and the four petticoats. A moment later she swayed away from him and wiggled out of her fancy lawn drawers. Abby kicked them aside and knelt beautifully nude on the bed beside him, showing not a flicker of embarrassment.

"Mr. McCoy. I think it's time we undid some of your clothes."

She undressed him.

A few minutes later they lay naked side by side on the bed.

She giggled and rolled over on top of him, and stared into his flint green eyes.

"Why?" he asked.

"I want to," she said and kissed him, her tongue filling his mouth, working his hot blood into a rolling boil. She drew back, grinning, pleased with what she was doing to him.

"I simply want to make love with you, and I'm used to getting what I want. I've learned how to persuade men to give me what I want."

Spur chuckled. "I bet you have at that." He pushed

her up and brought her forward so he could hold one of her breasts in each hand. Somehow it still wasn't right, but he couldn't figure out why.

He was in Abilene on official business: to investigate a problem the local authorities couldn't or wouldn't handle. Since the crimes involved crossing state lines, the United States Secret Service was called on to handle it. He had come from his base in St. Louis where he was agent in charge. His assignment here could have nothing to do with this classy lady. Spur reached up and nibbled at one of her swaying orbs and moaned in satisfaction.

She thrust her damp loins at him, and he felt her brush scratching across his erect manhood, producing a stinging excitement at its tip.

Abby pushed up so she could see his face clearly and stared at him, her green eyes darker now, worried.

"You are angry with me, Sweetman Spur. Troubled? Don't be. I am only what you see. I adored you from the second I saw you and I began scheming how I could attract you. At last I gave up that approach and decided to seduce you." She smiled and lowered a breast back into his mouth.

"Yes! Yes! Your chewing on me is marvelous! It sets me on fire. I want you now more than ever. But believe me, I really came here to look into the chances of starting a Harvey House Restaurant. But right now all I want is to make wild, fantastic love with you. And if you don't hurry up and show me a little bit of interest, I'm going to explode!"

Her face showed a testy, tantrum kind of anger

that amused Spur. She was just what she seemed to be, a woman who was as interested in sex as most men. It was a quality among women that he had seldom found in his extensive travels. Her swaying breast shifted and the other one lowered into his mouth as Abby purred softly over him.

Then Spur slipped over the edge, and quickly there was no right or wrong, no danger, no caution, only the searing flames of his desire, his billowing, surging need to have her, to experience her wondrous body in every way he could.

She remained over him, and now reached lower and helped a moment, positioning herself, then she pushed her hips downward, squealing a victory cry as his turgid flesh slid into her satin-lined sheath. Her natural cry of joy and desire pulled at him, tore at his consciousness, but he was too committed to evaluate or enjoy it. She gripped him inside with a steady rhythm that sent electric shocks of pleasure and pain through his loins. Then her small body surged into new action, her tight, womanly hips thrusting forward in a jolting sequence accompanied by a speeding up of the internal squeezing so he could measure the building of her desire.

His hands closed around her jolting breasts and he saw that her eyes were closed, a determined smile on her delicate features. Her breath came rapidly now, a gushing, warm panting. Sweat droplets spotted her forehead.

"Marvelous! So beautiful! I can't talk . . ." Her eyes widened and she moaned, then her hips speeded up and at last pounded with hard steady thrusts. She squealed and her head bobbed in counterpoint as she bent to seal her lips to his.

She broke off the kiss suddenly. "Omigod. Omigod. Omigod!" she wailed. "I'm going to die! I know I'm going to die! It's *never* been so perfect, so intense, so marvelous before. It's beautiful, just so damn fucking beautiful!"

She trembled and her face twisted into pleasure/pain as she spasmed in a jolting frenzy. Her whole body thrilled at her series of climaxes, rattling her like a rag doll, shaking her again as she endured a massive final contracting spasm. She melted against him, her breathing rapid and deep, as if she were unable to find enough air to gulp down.

She lay there five minutes. It was some time before Spur was aware that she was tightening around his hard shaft again, then releasing it in a cadence that gradually created the wildest, sexual feeling he had ever experienced.

"Poor baby, I forgot all about you," she said. "Your turn, darling. It's all your turn now, and Abby is going to help you do it so fine you'll never forget."

Gently they rolled over without losing touch. She lifted her legs onto his shoulders and smiled up at him.

"Hey, big, beautiful Spur. You've been here before. You know how fine it can be. And I have an idea anything I can do, you can do it much, much better."

He did. The hotel exploded into a million splinters of pine and cedar and they both sailed over the moon twice before landing again on her bed.

They lay there in each other's arms for ten minutes.

At last she stirred. Spur opened one eye. She was watching him.

"Nice, Spur McCoy, just tremendously *nice!* I feel delightfully well fucked." She giggled. "Sometimes I like to talk dirty. Hey, I invited you out to dinner. Do you suppose we're still hungry?"

"We are," Spur said.

A half hour later they settled into chairs at a wall table in the Drover Cottage Hotel dining room. There was white linen on the table, sterling silverware settings of six pieces and leaded crystal glassware. Spur could eat at the corner cafe all week for what a dinner cost here.

Spur watched Abby read the menu. When she selected the inch-thick roast beef he ordered the same. The wine was not the best Spur had ever sipped, but it complemented the meal.

Abby was wearing a prim, high-necked silk dress in soft blue, with wrist-length sleeves and a jacket that played down her marvelous figure. Spur felt pleased in a way. He didn't want to share her with anyone just yet.

"You never did tell me why you're in Abilene," she said.

Spur hadn't even thought of a cover story. He didn't expect he would need one to investigate why whole trail drive herds of cattle were being rustled. He almost stuttered but quickly recovered.

"My brother," Spur said. He was making it up as he went. "My brother Ken came out here two years ago and now he's vanished. Nobody knows what happened. Ken is steady and regular. He worked in the bank here. The family is upset, and I was elected to come and try to find him. It's not like Ken to take off, not even to tell his mother."

"He might have a good reason. Most folks who run off have their reasons, you know."

He nodded and they worked on the roast beef. It was cooked the way he liked: to a tender pink with savory juices and a dish of fresh ground horseradish and leeks that brought tears to his eyes. There was a jumble of cooked vegetables, lots of boiled potatoes and juices for gravy. Abby refused dessert, but Spur ordered a wide slice of fresh apple pie and a square of hard cheese.

"Mr. McCoy, this has been a fantastic afternoon. Really." Abby leaned closer and whispered. "But now I need to ask another favor. I want a bath and I don't have anyone to scrub my back . . ."

Spur laughed and shook his head. "That's an offer I never have refused before, but I have an appointment at a newspaper, the *Sentinel.* It might have something in it about Ken. It's the best place I have to start."

She frowned her displeasure. "I could throw a tantrum."

"You would have a good audience."

"But I would lose, right?"

"Right. I'd probably pick you up, lay you over my shoulder and carry you up to your room."

She laughed. "That might be fun too, only too public. It was too much to hope for." Abby lifted her finely plucked brows. "But I take a bath every night. Perhaps I could make the offer again tomorrow?"

Spur smiled and caught her hand. "I wouldn't at all be surprised that such a gracious invitation would be accepted with pleasure. And I might even have recovered my strength by then." He patted her hand and stood. "Now there's just enough time to get you back safely to your room before I run over and talk to that newspaperman."

CHAPTER 2

THE TRAIL BOSS STOPPED the herd an hour before sunset. The strung-out line of a thousand longhorns had smelled water an hour before and nothing could stop them from rushing to the small stream where they stood in the water. Some drank, some waited, some were gorged, two died. They drank so much they dried up the stream at a shallow and worked upstream. Soon all had taken on their twenty gallons and moved on across the small valley to be gathered into a "night clutch" by tired cowbows.

The men knew they were only twenty-five miles from the Abilene railroad stockyards, the end of the drive, payday, all the whiskey they could hold as well as all the women they could catch.

"I want two men on night-hawk," Riley said. He was trail boss, tall, thin, ragged, dirty and bearded after two tough months on the trail from Texas.

Three more days and they would be finished.

Pat Riley had heard things, rumors about whole herds vanishing, and the trail crew gone too. He hadn't believed them. But the closer he got to the railroad, the more careful he became. He assigned three men as night-hawks, just to make sure everything went right. The beef he had in his poke were worth four dollars each in Texas. At the rail stockyards they would bring thirty-five dollars each.

Thirty-five thousand dollars!

It was a fortune. A cowhand earned two hundred and fifty dollars *a year* if he was lucky. Riley and three partners had rounded up the beef in the wilds of West Texas. Strays. It took them a year. Almost nine thousand dollars each. He would have enough to buy a good spread in Texas somewhere and get a real start.

The cook had his fire going and the "Pecos strawberries," baked beans, ready by the time the crew came in for supper. The beans were in addition to the last of the sonofabitch stew that had been around for two days.

Riley rode around the bedded down beef, stopped on the far side and listened to the coyotes howl on the ridges to the west. He stared at the clear black sky and listened for the night birds. It was all there. Normal and natural, nothing out of place. Riley swore silently at his imagination and went back to the fire. He kept the fire going until after eight o'clock, then let it die out and rolled out his blanket, his head firmly on the rise of his saddle, his hand on his .44. Then he slept.

Out by the herd, Jeb Tally watched the campfire die to a glow as he made his rounds, walking his black horse slowly around the outside of the sleeping cattle. He wished he had been off night-hawk tonight but Pat had worries. Jeb worried when Pat did. He was a quarter partner in the herd. He'd gladly work another three nights if he had to to protect his eight to ten thousand dollars. Damn, what he wasn't going to do with that cash!

He turned suddenly. Had he heard something just beyond the herd? He was on the far side, close to the small ridge at the edge of the narrow valley and the row of trees. He shook his head. It had been a coyote. If it were daylight he'd use the critter for target practice.

Jeb turned around in the saddle and as he did a shadow behind him stepped from behind a gnarled cottonwood tree. The man ran quietly through the soft ground toward the rider. The slight figure wore a large Mexican hat and his right hand was cocked over his ear. Another five steps and his right hand slashed forward. The six-inch-bladed knife flew forward, spun once, and drove to the hilt in Jeb Tally's back.

Jeb knew he was hurt. He tried to call out but the blackness of night turned into white heat and he knew he was falling, only he thought it strange that he never hit the ground. As his consciousness faded away he realized he was dying and that he would go on falling forever through eternity.

Pedro Cruz pulled his knife from the dead man's back, wiped the blade on the corpse's shirt and slid the weapon back in its sheath. Then he hoisted Jeb over his mount's saddle and led the animal into the brush and over the ridge line.

Two more night-hawk men circled the cattle. Pedro killed the second man just before midnight and was moving toward the third when he heart a shot, a booming .44 that sounded from the camp.

Pedro drew his own pistol and sent two heavy slugs into the last night-hawk, then trotted toward the camp. He moved up as silently as a raven flying at dawn. When he was fifty yards away a voice called to him.

"Pedro! *Es bueno.* Come on in."

Pedro smiled and ran into the camp which now brightened as someone threw firewood on the coals.

Pedro made certain that it was Benjamin Hood building up the fire. He saw a tall, ragged man lying on his back near the fire. His face was a mass of blood. Pedro grinned and ran in.

"Don't stand there, you bastard Mexican cut-throat," Ben Hood bellowed. "We got bodies to bury deep and we got cleaning up to do. We're only three goddamned days from Abilene and they might have some lawmen out this far. Get your Mexican ass in motion!"

Pedro smiled. Ben Hood ran the gang, but they were equal share members, and already he had more gold and greenbacks than he thought existed in the whole *Estados Unidos.* He saw two other men dragging bodies from bedrolls toward a soft spot. The men began digging with long-handled shovels. When Ben said deep Pedro knew he meant six feet. And the wild man would measure the hole.

Pedro dug and sweated, but all the time he smiled. When he went back to Monterrey in Mexico this fall he would be a rich man. He would live like a landed Don. He would command respect, and he would marry the prettiest girl in town, a *young* pretty girl.

Back at the campfire, Benjamin Hood had stripped the papers he needed from a packet the last man to die wore hidden inside his shirt. The leather pouch contained agreement papers signed by four men, stating that they had rounded up the herd and agreed to take them to Kansas to sell and would split the profits equally.

Ben squatted by the fire reading the papers. There had been seven men on this drive. He had six men total, still enough for the short trip remaining. There was little chance they would meet anyone who had known the dead man, this Pat Riley. In three days they would be into Abilene, make the sale and ride out of town.

Ben nodded as Pedro Cruz came and looked toward the body of Riley.

"Hell yes, get the bastard out of here. He put up a fight." Ben admired him for that. Riley was probably a smart enough fellow. But nobody was as clever, smart, and crafty as Ben Hood. Who else had earned nearly twelve thousand dollars in two months? Twelve thousand goddamn dollars!

Three more herds, that would be enough. Then he would go to San Francisco on the new train and live like a rich man was supposed to!

Ben stood, tucked the leather envelope containing the herd papers inside his shirt and went to check on the hole. It had to be six feet deep, that was the secret. If the remains were never found, nobody could figure out what happened. He checked the diggers. The seven corpses lay to one side. None of their clothes or boots were worth saving. The hole was deepening slowly.

"Come on you rich men, dig faster. We got to have everything cleaned up and looking normal by dawn, you galoots know that. We don't play rich yet, we work out butts off!" To underscore his words, Ben jumped in the three-foot-deep hole that was six feet long and half that wide and began digging. A half hour later he climbed out. It was nearly deep enough.

When it was finished and they dumped the bodies into it and began shoveling in the dirt, they used rocks too, and humped up the material over the grave. Three men went for horses. They walked the animals over the mound pounding it down, then filled it again, and trampled it solid. In the morning they would drive fifty head of steers across the spot to make sure it looked the same as the rest of the area.

Ben Hood sat by the fire working on a silver flask of rum. He had picked up the taste when he signed on as a sailor for two years.

Lawson.

The name came again to haunt him. It had been their second job, the second herd they had rustled outside of Abilene two months earlier. It went easy right through the sale until a seventeen-year-old kid came around looking for Charlie Lawson, the real owner of the herd. The cattle buyer had pointed Ben out to him just after he collected his cash for the sale.

The kid was hobbling on a broken ankle and had stared at Ben for a long time.

"You ain't Charlie Lawson," the kid said.

Ben had nodded. "Damn right, son. Name is Chuck Lanson. Got to admit the name sounds a lot alike. Who's this other hombre?"

"Oh," the kid said, confused. "But didn't you just bring in a herd? The bunch with that old broken horned steer that was the leader?"

Ben laughed. "Son, you must be all mixed up. We come in two three days ago, can't rightly remember through all the whiskey. Told the buyer to hold my money for me so I wouldn't blow it down some fancy woman's crotch. Sorry can't help you none, kid. You best look some more for your friend."

"Friend? He was my boss, out of Texas. He owed me forty dollars for the drive. Broke my ankle three days out so he sent me in to get it mended. Said I'd get my whole pay."

"Herd probably got held up. We saw one outfit spooked over half of Kansas about two days out. Might have been this Lawson."

"Damn. Maybe I should go look for them."

"Maybe so, son. Maybe so."

The kid had hobbled off with the crutch. Ben got his men together and left town that afternoon. They rode fifteen miles down the tracks to the remains of a railhead camp overflowing with fancy women and whiskey. He let the men enjoy a three day binge.

That had been their only close call. A chance happening. Now, every time he went into Abilene he wore different clothes and different looking face hair. Once he even wore spectacles. But he hadn't seen the kid with the broken ankle.

The plan worked. Rustle the whole trail herd. Eliminate the entire trail crew. No witnesses. No one would miss the crew for a month, maybe two months, and by the time any investigation started, Ben Hood would have "retired" to a spacious flat in San Francisco, passing the time of life, investing his money and sampling those unquenchable California ladies. If only that damned kid hadn't broken his ankle they would have a perfect record.

He got up, put some more wood on the fire and make a check around the camp. Everything had to be perfect by dawn. No knife holes in blankets, no bloody equipment. The horses were never a problem. They were simply put in with the remuda and would be sold along with the wagon in Abilene. Chuck wagons were a drug on the market in a cow town, with many a good one selling for fifteen dollars in the summer. They cost more than a hundred dollars from the Studebaker Coach Company new.

Ben circled the whole outfit again, found a stray saddled horse and turned it over to his remuda man. It was almost three A.M. by the big dipper when Ben was satisfied that everything was slicked up, and he bedded down by the fire, leaving three men on guard duty. They would move the herd only six or seven miles the next day, timing it so they could get into Abilene near the end of the day when the buyers and counters would be tired.

Ben grinned as he thought about it. A thousand steers in this bunch. The price might be up to forty dollars a head. He wished thc idea had been his. Then he would be dividing $35,000 with his crew, not just $7,000. But it was still more money than he could make in a dozen years. He had nearly $12,000 safe in the bank. That was more than the average cowhand could earn in forty-eight years! Three more herds after this one and it would be enough. Just three more herds!

CHAPTER 3

SPUR McCOY SPENT an hour in the small newspaper office. The *Sentinel* wasn't much of a paper, four pages once a week, but it did have news. He read every story for the past two months. The editor, who was also the printer, could remember no item about rustling of whole trail herds. The small, thin man pushed back the green eyeshade and polished metal rimmed glasses.

"Sure, I've heard such tales. But when it comes to tying them down, getting the facts, there just aren't any. Some kid came in with the most plausible story, about how he broke his ankle three days out and was sent on into town to get it fixed. When the herd came in, a bunch of different cowboys were driving them. Leastwise so he said. But he was just a kid."

"Is he still in town? What was his name?"

"His name? Damn, that's been a month ago. Kid said he was broke, he didn't get his twenty dollars a month pay for the drive. Name? One I'd never heard before. What was it? Hey, he gave me a note, said if I ever heard anything . . . Where in blazes did I put it? Yeah, tacked it to the wall."

The man spun his chair around and searched the back wall which was plastered with small notes. He found it.

"Yeah, here it is. Ezra Boyce. Said he was sleeping in the livery and mucking out for eats. Don't rightly know if the lad would still be there or not."

"Probably isn't," McCoy said. "Oh, I'd be right pleased if you didn't noise this around. I'm trying to get some stories together for a dime novel. Don't want another writer to catch on to this idea before I get it to my publisher."

"Yes, I understand." The editor's eyes narrowed. "You a real novel writer? Always wanted to do one."

"Writing them is easy. Getting them published is the hard part. Why don't you write one and publish a chapter every week? Be good for your paper."

The newspaperman was still nodding in agreement when Spur left the small plant and headed for the livery, the name branded on his mind: Ezra Boyce.

Spur found someone cleaning out the last stall.

"Ezra?"

The boy looked up quickly, then the expectation faded.

"Yes sir."

"I hear you think your trail boss and crew were all killed back on the trail somewhere. Is that right?"

"Yes sir, but nobody will believe me."

"How about telling me your story over some supper? Looks like you could use a square meal."

A half hour later Spur knew everything the youth did. Ezra was certain the lead steer was the same one.

"After two months on the trail you get to know the lead critter," Ezra said. "That was one smart steer. Charlie Lawson, he was our trail boss and half owner of the herd, was gonna take old snaggle horn back to Texas with us to lead another drive."

Spur nodded. He didn't need to take notes, he remembered everything the boy had said including the description of the man who probably had taken over the herd. It had happened before, but never quite this close to the end of the trail. Three women in Texas claimed their husbands must have been killed the same way. The men never came home. Ezra was the best witness so far.

Spur gave him two gold double eagles, forty dollars, and told him to take a room at the cattleman's hotel and eat right. Then Spur headed for the second best source of information in any cattle town, the leading gambling, whoring, and drinking establishment.

That summer in Abilene it was the Silver Spur. McCoy liked the name and pushed through the batwing doors to a raucous, hard drinking atmosphere. Two trail herds just hit town bringing in twenty cowboys with a dozen desires spilling over one another. The girls here would know what went on better than the town marshal or the undertaker. Spur leaned against the wooden bar made of rough lumber covered by a cloth and ordered a beer. When the bartender set it down it was warm. In August the ice house was emptied.

He watched four girls working the cowhands. Some of the men had already taken a bath, others were fresh from the trail, dust, beards and all. A big sign over the stairway read: "No Bath, No Bed." Below it was a scrawled paper sign: "No Exceptions, this means *You!*"

One of the girls looked to be barely into her teens. She was tiny with a small figure, a pert, round face still with some of its baby fat, and a smile that made you forget everything else. When Spur waved a finger at her she left an unwashed trio of cowboys and walked over beside him.

"Well, aint' we spiffy, now? You're new in town." Her voice was light and sweet, so out of place in the whore-bar that Spur had to remind himself of the setting.

"Buy you a drink?" Spur asked. "Sarsaparilla of course?"

"Yes, but you pay for whiskey. Don't you mind?"

Spur started to say it was government money so why should he mind. Instead he shook his head. She called to the barkeep and got her drink, which cost Spur a quarter, and they went to a table near the back.

"We don't get many swells like you in here," she said. "Do you have a name?"

He told her. "And you?"

"Kitten."

"Kitten, that's it?'

"That's the only name I use. You *are* new."

She sipped her sarsaparilla. The dance hall dress had been cut down but was still designed to show cleavage that wasn't there. Her soft brown hair had been curled and pinned on top of her head. Blue eyes stared at him and for just a moment moisture touched their corners then vanished with a defiant blink.

"What the hell you staring at?"

"A pretty girl, I always like to look at pretty girl. Besides I need your help."

"That's a switch."

"Are you pledged?"

She nodded.

"How much?"

"Two hundred."

Spur winced. It was the usual method for getting girls for Western brothels and gambling halls. An agent in Chicago or St. Louis looked for professionals or women down on their luck, gave them twenty dollars cash, a new dress and paid their fare to a small town that was short on whores. The girls had to pay back the inflated "charges". Most of them were never able to pay off the pledge they had signed. They were bonded slaves for as long as their looks held up.

"Do you want it paid?"

"If you have to ask . . ."

"There is a chance. But I need to know a few things. Can we talk outside?"

She laughed. "I haven't been out those doors in two months but twice, and that was to go to a special Mass with two other girls. If I go through the front door with you it costs you a flat fifty dollars."

"Your bossman is a regular businessman."

"Bosslady."

"Figures. I'll make a pledge to you. You help me

find out what I need to know, and don't tell anyone, and I'll get your pledge paid off or beat down to the honest rate and get you out of here. Deal?"

"Why?"

"Because I need your ears."

"You a gambler, an outlaw, or a railroad detective?"

"No."

She shrugged slender shoulders. "What the hell! I ain't got nothing to lose. What do you want?"

He told her quickly what she should listen for. Anything concerning trail herds rustled intact and murdered crews.

She snorted. "Somebody's always talking about that. Oh, oh, looks like I have a customer. I'll do it for you."

"You go upstairs?"

"Lilly says I'm big enough, so I'm old enough. But I'm special priced. Fifty bucks and she has to watch, to protect me. She keeps a cocked pistol in her hand the whole time."

"I'm going to have to meet this Lily."

"That won't be hard, sir. I'm standing right behind you."

The voice came across clearly and with it a decided English accent. He turned around and found an English manor mistress, complete with light red-tinted hair, clear blue eyes and the softest peaches and cream complexion Spur had ever seen. She was two inches taller than Abby and four inches higher than Kitten's even five feet.

"The Mistress of the Manor, I presume?" Spur

said, bowing grandly from the waist, doffing an imaginary hat.

She gave a hint of a curtsy as her pleasant face broke into a smile.

"My, my, my! Manners in the middle of Kansas. I never would have believed it. Are you bothering my Kitten?"

"I hope not." Spur said watching Kitten walk away, her hips boyishly slender. "She is young, isn't she?"

"Yes, and precious and protected, but she's too expensive even for you." She paused, and Spur had a feeling she was evaluating him, checking out his income and his potential as an asset for her and her establishment. He must have won.

"May I buy you a drink, Mr. . . ."

He gave a curt head bow as he used to do in Washington when he was on the Senator's staff. "My apologies, Countess, my manners are mired in the sty. I am Spur McCoy, late of Washington, D.C."

She held out her hand and he took it gently.

"Charmed, Mr. McCoy. I am Lady Lily Stanwood. I'm afraid the countess title is a bit too much."

"Lady Stanwood, I am honored to meet you and would be delighted to have a drink with you."

Three cowboys at a nearby table broke up laughing. Lady Stanwood ignored them, led Spur to a back table and then changed her mind.

"It would be much more comfortable in my flat," she said. "Through here if you please." They passed through a velvet draped doorway and up a sharp incline of steps. At the top there was an apartment of four rooms. Two of them had peep holes that gave a view of the entire saloon below. It was decorated in what he guessed was traditional English furniture. She went to a cupboard and poured two shot glasses of whiskey and set them on a low teakwood table next to an overstuffed couch.

"Please sit down," she said. He waited for her to sit on the sofa and she smoothed the spot beside her. He took it.

"She seems so young," Spur began.

"She is but we have more important things to discuss. You, for example. You're new in town. What are you doing here?"

Spur sipped the whiskey. He hadn't tasted anything so good since he left Washington. He chuckled. "Direct, aren't you? If you must know I'm a writer, but why I'm in town is a dark secret. I write Western dime novels and do extremely well. That's about all I can say right now."

"My dear boy, you must know more about yourself than that."

"I'm over thirty years old, six feet two and I'd make the world's worst cowboy."

She smiled and sipped her drink.

"Now, what about you, Lady Stanwood? How come an English Lady is dropped in the middle of a Kansas plains cowtown?"

"Good fortune and a heart attack. My husband was establishing a cattle ranch and I was on my way here when he fell over dead one day. Bad heart. So I sold the land and cattle and opened up this establishment." She laughed. "When George was alive he said I was a little whore. I guess I finally proved him to be right." She sat primly on the edge of the sofa, her legs six inches from his. Her dress was floor length and tightly buttoned at wrist and neck under a froth of ruffles. He guessed she was about thirty-five, not beautiful but attractive.

She smiled. "Writers always make good lovers, I've found. Since you were talking to Kitten were you looking for . . . what shall we say . . . a good time?"

"A gentleman can hardly know how to answer a question like that, Lady Stanwood. On one hand if he says no. . . ."

"Oh, fer Christ's sakes, bugger, forget the gentleman shit, do you want to get fucked good or not?" She dropped into a cockney accent and it startled him. But he began to laugh and she laughed with him. By the time Spur caught his breath, Lady Stanwood had placed one hand on his leg and was working upward to his crotch.

"I'm known to get a bit direct now and again," she said. "What say, Lovey, you ever had a good piece of English ass?"

Spur shook his head and she caught his hand and put it down the top of her dress which she had opened to her breasts. There was nothing under the dress and his hand closed around a warm breast that throbbed at his touch.

"Coo, luv, now that's more like it. Our hair almost matches color, so luv, we have to kip it up at least once." She undid the rest of the dress buttons to her waist, then started opening his pants fly. She worked the magic and his shaft surged outward past the fabric.

"Luv, what a fine one! Hope you haven't been serviced lately."

"This afternoon."

"More's the pity. But Lily has a solution to that. The mouth is always better than the crotch anyway for a man I always say."

She bent and caught the hardened flesh, her mouth enveloping it, her teeth chattering up and down a portion. Spur McCoy moaned in sudden excitement.

A moment later she came away from him, pulled her dress off and her short chemise baring her firm pink-tipped breasts. She slid to the floor and motioned.

"Down here, luv, it's better on the fucking carpet."

Spur laughed and dropped to his knees, then she was on him, pushing him down, pulling his pants off, taking more of his shaft in her mouth than he had ever seen done before. He roared in pure sexual desire as she built his desire higher and higher. He forced her down and knelt over her, pumping away at the last and she closed her eyes and accepted all he had to give her.

Spur rolled away panting and she was right behind him, lying full length on top, holding him down, drawing satisfaction from his nearness.

Ten minutes later they dressed and she served him proper English tea with milk and lemon. He hated tea but drank it. She looked at a clock on the wall.

"Oh, damn. I have to run. A goddamned meeting. You stay here. I'll be back in an hour. You stay, hear? I'll have to freshen up some."

"I'll be downstairs talking to the trail hands. Gathering local color."

She smiled. "Don't forget, it's my turn next. I'll be back in an hour."

Spur went downstairs, slid through the velvet curtain and soon had a warm beer and began talking to a loud trail hand. Before five minutes had passed he wandered out the back door to the alley searching for the privy. He had just stepped inside when he heard a buggy enter the alley. Through a crack in the wood siding he saw Lily come out the back door and get in the buggy. So she did have a meeting! He watched it move down the alley to a kerosene lantern hung on a building. There Lily got out and vanished inside.

Curious, Spur walked down the alley to see if he could tell where the "meeting" was taking place. Lily's carriage had left. He stepped into the shadows when he heard another rig coming. A rotund man, shorter than average, wearing a black derby, emerged from the buggy and entered a rear door under the lantern. The buggy drove away. Over the door Spur could make out faint lettering: The words read: *Abilene Stockman's Bank.* He was about to leave when a third rig came into the alley, discharging a passenger at the same stop. The latest man was tall and slender, wore no hat but carried a silver tipped walking cane.

A short wait produced no more carriages, so Spur walked to the rear door of the Silver Spur and back to his warm beer. He listened to a dozen stories about life on a trail drive, but heard nothing about the dangers of anyone rustling the whole herd. Everything else was mentioned: Indians, the weather, swollen rivers, freak snow storms, and always the chance of a tornado and lightning.

"On my first drive I was soaked wet for six days before it stopped raining," one cowboy said. "My pants stuck to my saddle more times than not."

Spur moved from group to group, listening, tossing out a question now and then. But it was discouraging. Not a mention that rustlers were wiping out trail drive crews and taking over the herds. Was it really true? Spur wondered if the men were afraid to mention the possibility that such things were happening.

Spur ordered another beer. He saw Kitten twice more. She hadn't been upstairs, and he could hear her tinkling laugh. The men seemed to talk to her more like a daughter or sister rather than a dance-hall girl.

Before Spur knew it the evening was over and the big Seth Thomas was striking midnight.

Lady Stanwood had not returned from her meeting. Spur finished his tenth or eleventh beer and walked across the street to the Drover's Cottage Hotel. He was glad he had a room on the second floor. He didn't remember how many beers he had on top of the shot glass of whiskey. He wasn't adept at hard drinking and by the time he got the key in his door he was weaving.

Spur didn't bother to light a lamp, but dimly he realized there was a lamp already lit. He hadn't left one burning. He blinked and stared around and saw a long lump in his bed. Had he left a dummy blanket roll in his bed? No. A definite "no" came through his alcohol-fuzzy brain.

He sat on the bed suddenly before he fell down and the lump screeched and sat upright.

It was Abby Newland in a silky blue nightgown. She blinked, then smiled.

"I got lonesome in my own bed. Hope you don't mind sharing yours?" In one fluid motion she pulled the flimsy nightgown over her head. "Now I'm sure you don't mind." She leaned forward to kiss him and he fell past her, his eyes closing, his mouth dropping open, emitting a soft snore.

She stared at him a moment, then shook her head.

"Damn you," she said softly. "You went and got yourself drunk. Out looking for your brother were you? He wasn't in that whiskey bottle, tall friend."

She got up, slid back into the nightgown, then pulled off his boots, jacket, and vest. She left his pants and shirt on and covered him. Then Abby snuggled up against his back. It was good to go to sleep next to a man again.

CHAPTER 4

SPUR WOKE UP at five-thirty, as he did every morning no matter when he went to bed. A white film coated his lips and when he tried to swallow he gagged. All that warm beer. He felt a warmth beside him and looked over without moving. A tousled head of summer-wheat-straw blonde hair spattered the pillow.

Abby. She had decided to wait for him last night. He wondered if anything romantic happened? Spur slid out of the bed as gently as he could. Abby mumbled and turned over as she slept.

Spur took off his pants and shirt, wondering who had started to undress him, and pulled on well worn blue jeans, a blue checkered work shirt and a wide brimmed range hat of dark brown. He slid his stockinged feed into scuffed cowboy boots, and strapped on his .44 six-gun so it rode just low enough to be respectable without inviting trouble. He curled the sides of his hat, kissed Abby's cheek and slipped out the door carrying a blue denim jacket. It took him a few minutes to rent a horse and saddle at the livery, then he was out on the trail, moving toward a cloud of dust barely half a mile outside of town coming from the south.

This was the end of the Chisholm Trail, that lanced almost due north from Corpus Christi and Brownsville, Houston, Fort Worth and a dozen mid-Texas cattle raising locations to Wichita, Newton and Abilene. It was the beginning of an era, Spur figured. More and more cattle would come up the Chisholm and the other trails now being forged. Cattle would be king in the West for a long, long time. So right now was the time to stop this mass murder of trail drive crews.

Spur soon met the lead elements of the closest herd. Cowboys turned the beef into a long thin line so they could be handled easier at the counting station and the pens.

He talked with the trail boss for a minute, mostly to be sure he didn't look like the description of the leader of the murder gang, then he swung wide, around the strays and got back to the well worn trail south.

When he was past the last of the herd, Spur paused and let the dust settle, then stared south again. Kansas was as flat as ever, with a few rolling hills, some water courses, but no mountains or ridges or bluffs to mar the view. The sun had come up bright and warm, and not a cloud in the sky. He stared south and found what he was looking for, a cloud of dust hovering over the trail. It was a sure sign of another big herd working north.

Spur moved his black now, a mare with a white blaze on her head, with a deep chest and a lot of staying power. She was a quarter horse, bred for cattle work, and at home on any range. He settled into her gait and cantered for a half mile, then let her walk.

He guessed the next herd was about five miles down the trail. Spur had never worked on a trail drive. It was hard, dirty, long hours, and paid little. But he knew the routine.

There was roughly one rider for each 200 to 400 cattle on most drives. But you still needed five men to make even a small drive. The trail boss usually led out, marking the trail. Two point riders on each side of the lead animals kept them heading along the selected route. Swing riders and flankers were positioned along the sides to keep the animals in line and moving. At the rear the drag riders had the toughest job, picking up strays and pushing on the stragglers while trying to breath through the cloud of dust with the help of a bandana over their noses. The larger the herd, the more swing and flank riders, and the more dragmen.

In the mornings the cattle are bunched into a rough line and a lead steer sent out. He is followed by the others. The column narrows to a dozen head wide and stretches out. As the hours continue, the column lengthens more, and narrows to four or five steers wide.

Spur came to a slight rise on the edge of a stream

and looked south. The closest herd now was within sight, a long brown river of cowhide flowing toward him three miles away.

Beyond the cloud of dust he could make out two more distinct roiling dust palls stirred up by thousands of cloven hooves. With this many herds coming up the trail the second year, what would it be like here in ten years? The Chisholm trail would be worn ten feet into the prairie and four hundred feet wide. It would look like a Roman highway.

Spur kicked the mare into motion, walking her down the slope, then letting her run wide open for a quarter of a mile before he settled her down to a canter, then a steady walk. She drank at a feeder stream and then walked on south at a steady four miles to the hour.

Spur had learned about horses the hard way, one almost died on him. Now he knew the limits. Most horses could walk all day at four miles an hour. That's forty miles covered in a ten hour ride. A horse can lope or jog at six miles an hour, but not for more than a couple of hours at a time. A wide open gallop can last for only a half mile with most good horses, then they need a breather. To cover nine miles in an hour produces a winded horse, lathered up, and needing to be walked out and wiped down afterwards.

As he rode Spur wondered why he was out here. He could have stayed in Washington in a nice safe, comfortable office. But here he was swatting horse flies, fighting the sun, and sweating like a fat man on a Sunday School picnic.

Spur McCoy was much more than he seemed. He

had been born and educated in New York City, went to Harvard University and graduated in the class of 1858 at twenty-four. His father was a well-known merchant and trader in New York, and after two years with his father's firm, Spur joined the Union Army with a commission as a second lieutenant and advanced to a captain's rank before Lee surrendered. After two years in the army he went to Washington, D.C. as an aide to Senator Arthur B. Walton of New York, a long-time family friend.

Congress quickly became aware of a need for some type of federal law enforcement group. There was no agency or force that could apprehend a criminal once he had crossed a state line. Congress put together a law creating the United States Secret Service in 1865. The original purpose of the group was to discover and arrest counterfeiters who at the time were printing as much paper money as the government. Gradually the Secret Service agents were called on to do other federal business, since they were the only agency with enforcement personnel. Soon Secret Service men were handling a wide range of law enforcement problems, most far removed from currency.

Spur joined the new group shortly after it was formed, and served six months in the Washington office, then was sent to head the St. Louis branch. He was assigned to handle all cases west of the Mississippi. Spur McCoy was chosen from ten men because he was the only one who could ride a horse with skill, and had won the service pistol marksmanship contest. Both qualities were considered of prime importance in the western region.

Spur's immediate superior was General Wilton D.

Halleck, U. S. Army retired, who worked in the Washington headquarters and was second in command of the service.

Spur usually roamed the Western states and territories, and spent little time in St. Louis. He worked mainly through the coast to coast umbilical of the telegraph line.

He was unmarried and planned on staying that way. Spur had no wish to leave a widow and half-orphans if he met up with a problem some day that he couldn't handle. So far the Secret Service had lost six men, shot dead.

Down a slight rise and over near the bend in a small stream, Spur saw a chuck wagon. It would be the noon stop for the herd, and "dinner" as the trail crew called the noon meal. Spur rode down and waved at the cook, a grubby Mexican who kept his hand near a pistol on the hinged work table that he had swung down off the end of the chuckwagon.

"Morning. I'm looking for the Dennison herd, is this it?"

"No. Parker herd. Trail boss should be along soon."

"Mind if I wait?"

The cook grunted a no and kept on fixing the noon meal, which evidently would consist of beef steaks. Spur knew that a trail crew seldom ate beef. There was no way to keep it more than a day and a half, even if the night was cool. And a killed steer was like throwing forty dollars away.

The cook turned as he cut the steaks. "This critter broke a leg, had to shoot it. No sense letting it all go to the coyotes and buzzards."

It was the only thing the cook said during the next hour that Spur waited for the trail boss. When he showed up Spur saw at once that he could not be the one described as the leader of the gang of murderers. The man was tall, slight, and had an English accent. He was the son of a big rancher in Texas, an Earl straight from England.

"Have you seen anything unusual, like a band of six men riding near the trail?" Spur asked.

The trail boss slumped in the grass near the stream and shook his head. He dumped a pan of cold water over his head, letting it soak into his shirt and pants where it ran down. He shook his head like a wet dog and blinked away the wetness.

"England was never like this," he said, his accent broad. "No, I'm sorry, chap. We've seen nothing but trouble on this drive. Six hundred bloody miles, but it's almost done."

"We've been hearing about some rustling problems."

"Rustlers?"

"Yes. First the gang kills the whole trail crew, then drives the herd in and sells it. At least that's what we think has happened. Tell your men to be watchful these last few miles."

"Bloody bastards, we shall be careful. You must stay and have a steak with us. I bloody hate to see all that beef go to waste, but nothing else we can do. You say a whole trail crew murdered?"

They talked. Spur told the young man about Lily and he promised he would stop by and see her. They might have friends in common.

An hour later, Spur left. The next closest herd was six hours ride south, and then there were four more coming. The Parker herd had almost three thousand head and a ten man crew. The Secret Service man decided there was no point in riding out to warn the crews until he had some better information for them. He turned back toward Abilene and reached town an hour later.

Spur sensed a change as soon as he tied up his horse and walked down main street. There was a tension in the air. Men stared at him coldly as he walked by. Clumps of two and three men stood on the board walks and at the corners talking.

Spur went to the Sheriff's office and pulled open the door. A deputy whirled around, then relaxed.

"Hey, stranger, move slow around here. Everyone is a little jumpy."

"Why?" Spur asked.

"You ain't heard? That last trail crew that hit town told us. Trail boss brought in papers, guns, saddles, personal stuff. Said he found an open mass grave about three days out. Looked to him like somebody killed these guys, and dug them a deep grave. Only that gully washer we had about two weeks ago must have changed the course of a little river and it dug a ditch down through this meadow and cut right through the grave. Near as we can figure this bunch was a trail crew from Texas. Sheriff got the names and everything from some papers inside a waxed package. Sure as hell, a Texas trail crew. Guess we should have listened to that kid who said something like this happened."

Spur turned around and ran out the door. He had to talk to that trail boss again. He could get the names from the sheriff later. This was a break he had been hoping for. No wonder no one ever found the bodies. Dig them six-foot graves and run the herd over the spot, sell the horses with the others in the remuda. Simple, so damn simple and so goddamned hard to trace. Now all he had to do was find out who was doing it, and catch them at it.

Spur tried first at Lily's. He wasn't there. He checked two more saloons and found the drover at the Cattleman's Cafe, where a cowboy fresh off the trail could get a square meal for fifteen cents, even if he hadn't had a bath, shave or haircut.

The trail boss looked up, nodded and worked on a quarter slice piece of a cherry pie.

"Ain't had no pie in three months," the cowboy said taking another bite. Spur sat down across the table and nodded.

"The mass grave. I have a special interest."

"Done told the Sheriff."

"I'd appreciate it if you could tell me too."

The trail boss sighed, nodded. "Like I told the lawman, we must have been the first herd past there since the storm. River cut a new channel and dug through this little meadow and cut down eight or nine feet into the ground. One body was in the runoff channel. Rest was stacked like cordwood in the side of the hole.

"Looked like they dropped the corpses in first, then threw in their rifles, pistols, knives and then the saddles."

The cowboy took another bite of the pie. "I ain't

one much for being the undertaker, but I'd say them bodies ain't been in the ground more than two weeks. We checked them. Three was shot dead, and four was done with blades. Close work, messy, lots of blood."

The trail boss finished the pie and looked up. "Hell, that's about it. Story sure set this town a-jumping. Guess trail drives are important hereabouts."

"More than important," Spur said. "Thanks. Any idea how a whole crew could get jumped that way?"

"Yep. Night. Must have got most of them in their blankets. They was some blankets in the hole too, some with knife holes in them. They take out the crew sleeping around the fire, with their knives, all silent like. They they gun down the night riders on the herd. Easy. Then they move in, take the herd and waltz them in here, sell them and take off with all that money. Somebody else's money."

"Thanks, pardner," Spur said, and put a two dollar gold piece on the table. "Your supper is paid for."

Spur crossed the street and went up to the second floor room at the Drover's Cottage. He was stripping off his dusty clothes when he heard a knock on the door.

Spur walked to the door, his shirt in hand, and opened the panel a crack.

Abby Newland peeked inside. "Hey, you're back. You sneaked out on me this morning."

He pushed open the door and she glanced up and down the empty hallway, then slipped into his room.

"Looks like you're getting ready to have a bath," she said.

"That was my plan."

"Want to share? A shame to let all that hot water get used just once."

Spur laughed and bent to kiss her peppermint lips. When he stood again he was smiling.

"Share and share alike, I always say."

CHAPTER 5

THE DROVER'S COTTAGE Hotel had no bathrooms. For a bath you arranged to have a tub of hot water brought to your room. A half hour later a metal tub was half-filled with steaming water.

Spur sat down on the bed and clasped his hands behind his head. "Ladies first," he said with a teasing grin.

Abby shook her head. "It's too hot, and I'm too cold. How would you like to help me solve that problem?"

"What do you mean?"

It was a ridiculous question and he knew it. She wore a soft white silk blouse he knew must have cost a month of his pay. She turned quickly and when she faced him the blouse floated gently to the floor and her firm breasts were free, uncovered, and swayed and bounced with her body's motion.

She ran to him and pushed him backwards on the

bed, sat on his stomach and laughed as she unfastened his belt. She jumped off the bed and pulled off his boots, then his pants. A moment later he was naked and she watched his crotch and the steady growth and transformation that took place.

"I always have liked growing boys," she said with a giggle.

Spur scowled. "Ma'am, that's no boy." He pulled on her skirt, a heavy cotton, and it came down quickly. She wore nothing under it. She twirled around for his inspection.

"Did you know I studied to be a ballet dancer?" she asked. She did a series of pirouettes, stopping gracefully with her hand on his shoulder and rising on her toes, then spun away from him in a half dozen bouree turns on half toe. "But then I got bored and I got too fat. Ballet dancers are dedicated and they never eat at all."

"The bath?"

"Together," she said.

"We both can't get in that little tin tub."

"We can't sit down in it but we both can stand in it."

Spur marveled at her perfect body, her heavily nippled breasts surging forward, and her slender, graceful legs. She *was* a dancer. Then she was against him, pushing her body tightly to his, her arms locked around his bare back. She nibbled at his chest and laughed softly, then licked his nipples until he yelped.

"My turn," she said, and licked them again. She reached up to be kissed. His arms wound around her and he kissed her deeply, his tongue a flame inside her. He suddenly wished he was inside her in another place.

She twisted away.

"Now, now, we need that bath first, you're positively . . . dusty!"

She stepped into the tub of water and got out again. "Scalding!"

He tried it and found it warm, but not that hot. Soon she stepped in beside him and they were forced to stand close together.

"Wash my back," she said.

He shook his head. "I'd rather wash your front." Spur bent, found a bar of soap on a chair, and began lathering her breasts, her tight little belly and the swatch of brown fur lower down.

Giving a beautiful girl a bath was one of Spur's favorite pastimes, and he made the most of it, lathering and relathering until she turned around suddenly and he washed her back.

As she turned she caught the soap and began lathering Spur's chest, then his crotch. There was no way Spur could prevent a full erection and her ministrations hurried the process. As he came rigid and bold Abby giggled. She lathered him again and made him turn around.

Spur let her wash his back, then spun around and bent to chew on her soapy breasts. It didn't matter. He needed her again. He wanted to pick her up and throw her on the bed, soap and all.

When he did Abby yelped in surprise. His hands slipped on her round soapy bottom, but he dug his fingers into her buttocks and carried her to the bed. Spur dropped Abby and stared down at her. Her hands caught her soapy breasts and she caressed herself, thrusting her peaks upward toward him. Then she pushed her hips upward, her legs spread and her soapy crotch beckoned him. He started to lower himself but she shook her head and jumped up to her hands and knees and pushed her round behind toward him.

Spur groaned deep in his throat as he knelt behind her. Abby's head turned and she looked over her shoulder, smiling and nodding, urging him on.

He knelt and probed and then slid into her velvet sheath to Abby's moan of acceptance and delight. She moved against him in a small dance and as he began to work back and forth they established a cadence that set his nervous system on fire. She jolted against him and before he realized it, Abby was growling and clawing at the bed, slamming against him harder and harder until she melted and slumped.

Her climax pushed him over the edge too, and he exploded a dozen times.

He lay there panting and in a moment she was all over him. Her tongue licked him, her teeth nibbled at his chest, his hips, his face. Spur tried to tell her he was through for six hours at least, but he couldn't convince her. Her tongue became a searing branding iron that set him on fire each time it stroked him. Within minutes he was erect again and clawing at her soapy body. She pushed him down and sat astride him, then slowly, gently lowered herself onto him, sliding his lance deeply into her opening, settling on him for the deepest penetration possible. Only then did she moan some words low in her throat, a half-savage, half animal cry of satisfaction, of a need fulfilled.

Abby began to rock gently at first, gradually increasing the pace and the thrust of the rocking motion until it ignited another raging fire deep inside her partner.

She leaned upward and looked down at Spur, her hands on his shoulders. She smiled warmly with a spontaneous delight that made him swell with pride.

Her tempo had increased. She was riding him now like a pinto pony, and her head went back and she gave a soft cry of victory, of dominance, of total joy.

Spur wasn't thinking about the fine points. He had dissolved himself into the stark, frenzy of her passion.

Her wild ride continued with abandon, yet with a caressing delicate skill. Each surging downward stroke of her hips melted the pair into a peaking moment of rapture. When she raised herself, pulling away from his shaft he died a little, afraid that she was going to leave him, but the terror lasted only a moment. Abby came plunging back down and he stabbed deeper and deeper into her.

Her climax came suddenly, surprising him.

"Oh, god, I'm dying! Help me, save me, I'm dying! I know nothing has ever been so sweet, so marvelous, so wonderful, Spur. I'm dying, do something!"

He gave one last thrust of his hips and shot into the heavens. Then she rolled away, panting, pounding the bed with her fists.

They rested, wiped the soap from their bodies, and came together again, gently, softly, with great emotion, sharing and tenderness. They had found it all, savage love as well as tender, beautiful passion.

She dressed him slowly wanting it to last as long as possible.

It was nearly dusk when they stared out the window at the beginnings of a cattle town, a cattle drive Kansas cattle-pen town. For as long as it lasted.

She sat naked on the bed and watched Spur finish dressing.

"Let's have dinner and then play cards in my room," she said.

He shook his head. "Business. I have to talk to some people about my brother."

"You'll do it in a saloon and get drunk again," she said, the start of a tantrum blossoming.

He caught her round face in his hands and kissed her.

"Not true. I do have to look in the saloons. Men there know a lot, and liquor loosens their tongues. I'll be back early."

"Supper?"

"We can have a late supper."

Spur went across to the Silver Spur saloon and looked for Kitten. The apron said she was probably upstairs. Spur listened to the talk. The betting was that whoever killed the trail crew had been paid off and gone out of state by now. They would never be found, and there might even be more mass graves out there along the trail. Spur silently agreed: the killings probably had happened more than once.

Kitten came down the stairs brushing hair out of her eyes, trying to look grown up and brave. It didn't work. She seemed angry, scared, and half sick. Spur met her at the bottom of the steps and took her to a table.

"Spur, I think I'm going to die."

"You probably feel like it. But dying is no damn fun at all."

She looked up sharply. "Don't make fun of me, I hurt."

"It shows. And I'm sorry. But hurts get better. You will too. I need some help from you. What about your bosslady? You know much about her?"

"Some."

"She went to a meeting last night." He described the men and the place.

Kitten snorted. "Ha! They think they're going to run Kansas. The Big Four, she calls them. She drinks now and then, and one night she bragged to me about it. Said she had the three of them eating out of her hand. Probably the other way around. One of the three is our banker, Nance Victor. Then there's the gent with the silver headed cane. His name is Dennis Gundarian, runs the Emporium, Abilene's only general store and haberdashery. The other one in the derby has to be Hans Kurtzman. He's putting up a new hotel, and Joe McCoy is mad as hell about it. Those four are always planning something, but nobody is supposed to know anything about it. They are never seen together during the day."

Spur toyed with his warm beer and frowned. He could see no connection between the Big Four meetings and the murder of the trail crews.

Kitten smiled up at him. She seemed to be feeling better.

"I made twenty dollars just tonight," she said. "Some big spenders in town. I have my bondage down to a hundred and eighty dollars. I thought it was lower than that. But Lily said something about five percent interest a month. What's interest?"

Spur growled and hit the table. "It's a way Lily will use to keep you in her place forever. I'll talk to her about that."

He looked into his beer. Kitten could wait. What he needed now were more details. If the trail drive kid, Ezra Boyce, could remember more about the leader of the trail crew that took over his herd. Spur stood quickly, almost spilling his beer.

If the kid was still in town!

He patted Kitten on the shoulder saying he would be back. He hurried out the front door to the Cattleman's hotel, a rickety establishment that had been thrown together quickly by the town's founder while the Drover's Cottage was being built. Rooms were a quarter a night if you brought your own blankets. The man at the desk said Ezra Boyce was in 208, upstairs.

Spur ran up the steps two at a time, hoping the young man had not slipped out and headed for Texas.

There was no answer to his knock. Spur tired again then grabbed the doorknob and turned it. The door came open and Spur saw there was no light. He slipped inside and dug out a pack of "stinkers," tore off one and lit it. The phosphorus cardboard match flared into light, then steadied.

Spur saw all he needed to in the ten seconds before the match burned his fingers.

Ezra would never testify against anyone. He lay on the bed, a large pool of dry red blood caked around his neck. His throat had been slit from ear to ear.

Spur eased out the door after making sure the dimly lit hall was empty. He walked down the back stairs and into the alley. Someone had made sure Ezra would never testify or give information about the killers. But did that mean the mass murderers had been in town during the last day or two? And how would they know that the boy had been talking? Who had he talked to beside the Sheriff and Spur McCoy?

CHAPTER 6

SPUR McCOY WENT to every saloon in town that night, listened to the talk about the trail crew massacre. Although everyone had a theory none of them held up. Spur gave up about ten o'clock and went back to his room. The bathtub and water were gone. The wetness wiped off the wooden floor, the bed made and a disgruntled Abby Newland sat cross-legged on the bed in her silk nightgown playing solitaire with a new deck of cards.

"At least you're sober," she said bouncing up. "Find out anything about your brother?"

"No. Nothing. He's just dropped out of sight."

"Let me help you. I've seen what I came here to find out. Let me help you find your brother."

"No, it might be dangerous."

"I've been in dangerous situations before."

"I bet you have." He stared at her a minute, then sat down on the bed and pulled off his boots. She tried to kiss his ear, but he pulled away.

"A time for everything, Abby. And right now it's time for me to sleep, alone. I've got a long ride coming up tomorrow, bright and early."

She nodded. "Spur McCoy, you're not here looking for your brother are you?"

He watched her.

"I know you're not. I talked to both the newspaper man and the sheriff. You're working on the trail-drive crew murders. Why didn't you say so? Maybe I can help."

She knew. There was no use lying about it.

"Thanks, but I work alone." He unbuttoned his fly and kicked off his pants.

"Sometimes a matched team pulling a rig can do so much better."

"People in my line of work get killed. No way I'm exposing you to anything like that." He bent and kissed her cheek. "Now, I need some sleep. You want to sleep here, fine, just don't attack me in the middle of the night. Deal?"

"Deal." She grinned and began pulling off her silk nightgown. "Too hot to wear that thing," she said and lay down naked on the sheet. "I won't even touch you."

He took off his shirt and lay down beside her. Christ, this was never going to work. He leaned over and kissed her cheek.

"Goodnight," he said.

"Nite."

She lay on her back staring at the ceiling as he blew out the kerosene lamp. He tried to relax. Her hand curled over his shoulder. She nestled against his side and in a minute she was breathing evenly.

Spur grinned to himself in the dark, tightened the muscles in his body and relaxed them one by one. By the time he worked down to his toes, he was sleeping.

Spur had an early start and was almost five miles out of town heading south on the trail when the sun came up. He stopped for a drink from his canteen, then moved the black mare south again. He had decided the best way to check out the herds was to meet them as they came toward Abilene. Within three days drive of the town he should find four or five outfits. He might get lucky and spot the man Ezra had described. Probably not. If he went more than four days out he would be spending too much time in the saddle.

He hit the first herd six miles south. The men were feeling good, thinking about their first real bath in two months. Then there would be a shave and haircut and a real saloon with working girls, whiskey and gambling.

Franz Wilhoit, the trail boss, was short, stout, with a clean-shaven face that had been sunburned to a ruddy glow. This was his third trail drive and there wasn't a chance he was the killer. Franz insisted Spur have a mug of coffee and bowl of stew before he left. The herd would be in for an early dinner in about an hour. Spur thanked him and pushed on, went upwind past the Longhorns and caught sight of the next dust six miles back. By the time Spur found the chuck wagon of the next outfit, the cook hadn't yet set up for the noon meal. He was fuming, waiting for the trail boss to pick a spot. When the head wrangler came in he was tired, angry and bone weary of pushing steers and men around.

"Last goddamned time I lead a herd anywhere!" he fumed. "Cows is the contrary king, and ornery on top of being bovine stupid!" Then he grinned, grabbed a cup of coffee the cook had made over a temporary fire. "Damn, I say that everytime I get about this far. But I always hire on again." The man was the right size and age, but somehow Spur couldn't see him as a bushwhacker, not a cold-blooded killer who struck from the dark and killed men in their sleep.

Spur finished his coffee and moved on. When he came to a small rise over a river he stared south. He could see only one dust cloud.

Spur rode for the rest of the afternoon and failed to meet a third herd. At dusk he made camp near a small stream, rolled out his blankets and built a small fire for coffee. Spur built a ring of rocks around his cooking fire, set a tin can on the rocks until the water heated, then dumped in a palmful of ground coffee and let it boil for five minutes. It would be strong enough to stand by itself—just right.

As Spur lay by the fire and listened to the night birds calling, he went over what little he knew about the trail herd rustlers. He simply didn't have enough facts. If he identified the killers out here he would ride quickly north and meet them at Abilene with a posse of fifty men. But the chances of running into the killers with a herd were slim.

Spur let the fire die down, watched the stars overhead, and relaxed. This was a part of his job that he never tired of, peaceful nights in the outdoors, without another human being for miles, and no one but himself to rely on. It was a heady feeling.

As he drifted off to sleep, Spur wondered how many crews had been wiped out just three or four days from Abilene. Could it be two? Maybe ten or twelve? There might be no way of ever knowing. Dammit, he would find out, he had to!

It was almost daylight when Spur came awake. He wasn't Indian alert but he knew someone was in his camp. He didn't move, nor open his eyes. Furiously he tried to remember on which side he had put his .44. The right side when he was on his back. In one sudden move he opened his eyes and grabbed for his weapon.

A black, unpolished, weather-beaten boot slammed down on his wrist pinning it six inches from the .44.

"I'll be a fucked-out whore's momma," a drawling voice said over him. Spur looked up at a tall, thin man in ragged rugged blue pants and a tattered shirt. He was bearded and dirty, with long scraggly hair and beard but most important, he had a six-gun aimed squarely at Spur's right eye.

"Wall now, 'pears we got a live 'un, Cissy May. You said keep him 'live so shore 'nuff he'ens still 'live."

"Chris' sakes, let the poor boy up, pa. Don't look none dangerous to me nohow. Stand up, big man, cat got your voice box?'" Spur couldn't see the woman. He turned to look at her. But the man slammed a kick into Spur's side and spun him around. Spur almost gagged. Fortunately the blow had been too high to hit his kidney area. He sprang to his feet and got a good look at the pair. Just as he did a rifle bullet spanged away off a rock between his feet.

"Easy, Boy!" the man called. "We want this one live. Promised you old ma."

Spur could see the man and woman now. She was short, pudgy with a little girl face crusted with grime, her brown hair had turned into matted strings and she wore the remnants of an old robe.

"Business first, Pa," the woman said. "Boy up in the rocks will cover you with the long gun. Get his purse. He must have a big wad of Yankee bills, maybe even some good money."

The man with the pistol spun Spur around and jerked a folding leather wallet from his hip pocket. There should be plenty of money there to satisfy them. Spur knew at once they weren't the trail herd killers. There was no woman with them, and a man with such a heavy drawl would have been remembered.

"Wheeeeeee Ha!" the man screeched. "Must be three, four hundred dollars in here, Cissy May! Yankee greenbacks but we can get something for them. And ten gold double eagles, that's a lot more."

"Two hundred dollars, Pa," a younger voice called from the left and above them.

"I knew that!" the man snapped.

"Now, business is over," the woman said. "Give me the fucking money, Pa, just like always. Hold a six-gun on the peckerhead whilst I get the money hid. Then bring in Boy."

The cadaverous looking thin man did as the woman ordered, with no show of anger or question. Cissy

May vanished behind Spur and ahead he saw a boy, not more than fourteen, come out of the brush, a vintage muzzle loader in the crook of his arm. He was tall and slender with pimples on his face and his hair cut short so it stood straight up on top. His big ears looked out of place and when Spur saw the light blue eyes and shy grin, he knew that Boy had problems.

"Do I get to watch this time?" Boy shouted although he was six feet from them.

"Hush up your ugly mouth!" his father bellowed and backhanded Boy across the mouth knocking him down. As he got up, the youth pointed the old rifle at the thin man. Spur tensed but the man countered with a high, thin laugh, looked away, then with a sudden move slapped the rifle away and backhanded the boy again.

"Don't never point that thing at a body unless you aim to do them serious harm, little bastard. Done told you that a dozen times. Drop your pants, Boy."

"No, Pa. Don't make me. I sorry. Don't make me!"

"Drop 'em!"

The boy undid his belt and let his pants down.

"Bend over you dumb assed whelp!"

The boy bent over so his white buttocks showed in the morning sunlight below his torn shirt. Twice the man cracked his three-inch belt across the white moons and the boy wailed in protest.

"You done it again, Pa, Boy done got himself a harder," Cissy May said, giggling as she watched the youth try to cover himself.

"Hail, he's got a harder half the time." The man shook his head. "Boy just got to learn." He turned dismissing the sobbing youth and looked back at Spur. "What the hail we gonna do with the big one. You still want him?"

"Sweet lord in heavens, I almighty do! I ain't passing up this one. We ain't got no hurry, stay here half the day if'n we need to."

"Yeah, Cissy May, do him so I can watch," Boy said.

The man roared with anger and chased the boy around Spur's camp. "You unnatural whelp! God-damned strange, queer boy! You'll be the death of me yet!" He caught the boy who had tripped and fallen. The thin man's boot whacked into Boy's side twice. As he screeched in pain he smiled. Both his hands were holding his crotch.

"Stop it, Yorst, you know the little peckerhead likes it." She turned toward Spur and he could smell her coming. He figured she hadn't had a bath in months. When she grinned he saw half a dozen blackened stumps of her remaining teeth. "Now, little bigger boy, let's see what you're hiding in them britches. Oh, don't worry, I'll take care of you *good.*" She cackled with glee. "I always takes care of the big range bulls like you. I'll get you interested a little."

Cissy May opened the top of the tattered wrap around and let one massive breast swing out and sag onto her stomach. She laughed and exposed the other breast and tied the arms of the garment around her large waist and moved closer to Spur.

"Now, little Honey Boy, does that give you some ideas? Do them big ones rile up your gonads a mite?"

Spur backed away and the six-gun in the man's

hand thundered a lead messenger behind him. He stopped backing up.

"Son that's a mite better," the tall, thin man said. "You just settle down and let Cissy May have her way with you and we can get this over with and on the move. Shit, you're even gonna enjoy it. Cissy May might be a little heavy but she sure as hell knows how to use all of it!"

"Kneel down, Honey Boy, so I can get a good look at you," Cissy May said. Almost at once Spur felt something club him in the back of the knees and he jolted forward to both knees. Cissy May caught him and one huge, pink breast swayed directly in front of his face. The areola was three inches across, a deep brown and the nipple was a darker brown. Now the nipple had extended and risen so it was a half inch long. Spur stared at her nipples in surprise.

"Honey Boy, have a bite, chew on me some, that always gets me started right." She thrust one breast against his face and Spur's mouth opened by instinct. As he mouthed the breast he felt it throbbing with excitement.

At last Spur got his thoughts gathered together. There had been little time to do anything but react and stay alive since he woke up.

Rawhiders! They had to be one of the small bands of vicious cutthroats who roamed the wilds, preying on anyone they found. He had seen the results of several encounters. The rawhiders moved in, robbed, raped the women, then killed everyone. They took all the property they could including horses, wagons, sometimes furniture to sell, and moved on to the next victim. The Secret Service was concerned about the bands, but they were so fleeting, that it was hard to stumble across them, let alone try to go out and hunt them. Now Spur had a classic case with himself as the victim. It would make a great report if he lived long enough.

The woman was talking and Spur concentrated on listening to her.

"That's a sweet boy, Honey Boy. Oh, yes, we gonna have ourself one fucking good time. You'll get so hot and bothered you'll just make love all morning. Hell yes, we can make it last three or four hours. You're a strong one. About six times, I'd guess, unless you lose too much right at first."

She unbuttoned her shirt and stripped it off, then pushed her other breast into his mouth.

"We got to even up. Sweet over here got all the chewing, now help out Miss Sour." Cissy May laughed and untied the robe around her waist. Spur saw it slipping down. At first he thought that she was wearing something under the robe, then he realized that she had on nothing at all under it. Her fat belly almost met with her sagging breasts, as it billowed out in rolls of fat that hid even the hint of a crotch. When she moved the fat shook like a bowl full of crab-apple jelly.

Cissy May whimpered and then groaned. "Christ, now you're getting me hot as a pistol. It's supposed to work tother way." She pulled away from him and rubbed his chest with both hands, then down to his belt.

"Stand up, you big fucker, let's see the rest of you."

Spur looked at the thin man with the .44. The rawhider grinned and waved the weapon.

"You best do like she says, then she won't cut your balls off."

As Spur stood he saw that the boy had dropped to his knees, his right hand was pumping hard at his crotch. A look of total ectstasy filled the boy's face.

"Well now, fancy damn belt buckle," Cissy May said as she pulled the belt out of his loops. "Can get me fifty cents for that at the next little town." She opened the buttons on his jeans and pulled them down, taking the short underwear with him.

Spur had no erection.

"Sonabitch, I ain't even got you a harder yet!" She began kissing around his genitals, then caught one of his hands and pulled it up to her crotch. Spur looked at the long-haired man.

"Doesn't this bother you, even a little?"

"Hail no, you dumbbell. It's the throw of the dice. Last week I had me three sisters, sixteen to eighteen. Hail, that was my turn for three days. I got me so fucked out I couldn't travel for a day. This here is Cissy May's turn."

When the man finished talking, Spur watched the muzzle of the pistol wave at him from three feet away.

"Hey, you sonbitch, you get it hard for the lady, or I'll have to blow a hole in your kneecap. You ever get a kneecap shot up before?"

"Nope," Spur said. Out of the corner of his eye he saw the boy groaning and moaning as he pumped.

"Look at that!" Spur said nodding at the boy. The

instant the man's glance went to the boy, Spur swung his right arm, his fist backhanding the rawhider along the jaw, jolting him sideways and spilling the six-gun from his hand.

Spur pushed the naked woman away, spun and kicked hard with his right boot. His aim was perfect as his foot crashed into the rawhider's crotch, smashing his testicles against pelvic bones, crushing both of them. A shrill scream of tormented rage gushed from the man's throat as he pivoted to one side, dropped to the ground and pulled his knees up to his chest, screaming in agony.

Cissy May dove for the pistol and Spur stepped on her hand, grabbed the pistol and turned. The boy had caught the action. He deserted his erection, grabbed the musket and bolted into the brush. Spur ran the other way putting some distance and protection between himself and the powerful, if slow shooting, vintage weapon.

Spur slid behind a large cottonwood and peered cautiously around it. He could see his camp. The woman sat where she had fallen, nursing her bruised hand. She hadn't dressed. The thin man still writhed on the stretch of sand near the little stream.

The boy vanished with the rifle. Spur had to dig out the boy and disarm him.

"Hey. Boy. I've got no fight with you. You can come in and get your people and leave. I won't hurt you or them."

"The hail you won't!" the boy called.

The silence came and stretched out. Spur was about ready to try sneaking up on the boy, when he decided to talk instead.

"I saw how they treated you. Are they your real parents?"

"Hail no! I'm an orphan."

"But you shoot straight."

"Hail yes! Watch the old man's arm."

A shot boomed from the brush and the rawhider's arm jolted with a round ball and he bellowed in pain and rage.

"Now watch his legs," the boy called. Spur was moving. Unless he was an expert it would take the boy a full minute to reload the muzzle-fed weapon. Spur ran through the fringe of brush and slipped through a screen of willow. He saw the boy for a moment but he moved and a few seconds later the musket roared again. Spur jumped up and ran directly for the sound.

He was almost too late.

The tall youth had the blank powder loaded and the ball almost seated when Spur slipped up behind him and put a pistol against his ear.

"Drop the musket," Spur roared. The boy let it fall without thinking. Spur picked it up and pushed the youngster to the ground. He looked out at his campsite and saw the naked woman sitting in the sand holding the man's head in her lap. She was crying.

"You killed him?"

"Damn right. He's pushed me and whipped me too much. I told him I'd shoot his ass some day."

"You have a team, a wagon, horses?"

"Yeah, one ridge over."

Spur remembered that his own pistol was still in the camp below. Spur watched the woman. She seemed totally involved with her grief.

"Can Cissy May shoot?" Spur asked.

"Damn good," the boy said. "She taught me."

Spur stood and yelled toward the camp. "Lady, you want to walk away from here, I'll let you go. Do it right now."

For a moment there was no reaction, then a sun-flash warned Spur and he dove for cover just before a pistol bullet sang through the air over his position. He rolled out of sight.

"Boy," Cissy May called. "Hey, Boy, I'm talking to you. If'n that big bull ain't got you by the scruff, you come on in. You and me can take him any week. You come running in and we gonna find our gear and get moving."

Spur had not forgotten the boy. He simply wasn't there. He had vanished.

A moment later Spur saw the lad race out of a stand of brush.

"I coming, Cissy May!" the boy screeched as he ran toward her.

The woman lifted Spur's six-gun and shot the boy twice at twenty feet. Both slugs hit his chest, mashing up his lungs, dropping him into the dirt where he rolled over gasping for breath until he died less than a minute later.

Three. She had fired three rounds, so she had only two left in his .44. Spur worked his way closer, found good cover and called to her. She didn't fire at his voice. He hoped she would burn up her last rounds.

"Cissy May, I'm going to have to arrest you for killing that boy. I'm a United States peace officer."

"Go to hell, or come along with me."

"I'm coming in, lay your weapon on the ground and stand up."

"Come ahead."

As Spur looked around the tree he saw that she had his six-gun up and held it with both hands. She sat in the sand with the dead man's head on her lap.

"I told you to put down the gun."

"Sure as hell did. And I told Boy I wouldn't hurt him. He didn't hurt much. Now I'm gonna kill you."

"You used up your last round. That's my weapon and I only had four rounds in it."

"Bullshit. I only fired three times."

"Try it and see."

"I'll try it when I kill you."

Spur knew she could shoot. He ran from one tree to the next, dropped and rolled once on a long stretch hoping she would fire, but she didn't. He got as close as he could without making himself a target.

"It's all over Cissy May. You can't run the wagon without the men. Give it up."

"And sit in some state prison for twenty years? Not me."

Spur settled down behind the tree and kept talking. He explained her chances every way he could. He told her how women's prisons weren't as bad as they used to be. Some didn't even have bars, just rooms. After a half hour she put the pistol in the sand.

"Shit, come and get me. Can't be any worse than this. Come on before I change my mind."

Spur kept his gun out as he lifted from beside the tree and started across a fifteen-foot-wide section of the stream bed. There was no cover at all. He watched the weapon in the sand and moved cautiously.

He was almost halfway across when Cissy May screeched and grabbed the pistol. Spur was twenty feet away. She lifted the weapon and before she could fire, Spur dove to the sand and rolled, coming up with his weapon aimed at her. Cissy May had followed him. Spur watched her face, hoping that he would be able to tell a fraction of a second before she was going to fire.

Her nose quivered, and then she squinted her right eye.

Both guns went off almost at once, but Spur's was quicker. His round struck Cissy May a millisecond before she pulled the trigger. Spur's round slammed through her heart, ending her rawhiding days and her life. Her round screamed an inch over Spur's head.

He lifted up and dashed foward. She was dead by the time he got to her.

Spur McCoy sat in the warm sand of the dry part of the stream bed staring at the three corpses. It didn't have to end this way, but it did. Cissy May must have hated Boy for killing her man.

It took Spur an hour to find the rawhider's rig. It had two horses, and a half-covered wagon loaded with clothes, silver goods, trinkets, a strong box and dozens of pieces of jewelry. There was also a shovel. Spur took the shovel back and buried the three bodies. He tied the two horses to the tailgate and headed the lumbering wagon toward Abilene. He had been out almost twenty miles and found nothing that looked like a lead on the trail herd killers.

It took him an extra day to make it back to Abilene, and he got in just as the sun was going down.

Spur drove the wagon up to the sheriff's office, told the deputy on duty what had happened and put the messy business in the hands of the county.

Back at the livery he turned the rawhiders' horses into the corral, brushed down his mare, hung up his bridle and then the saddle. He looked up as someone came into the dimly lit stable. Two men stood across from him in the flickering light of the stable lantern.

"Spur McCoy?" a voice said.

Spur felt he should know it, but couldn't place it. "Right, that's me."

He heard two six-guns cock and he tensed.

"This is Sheriff Zedicher, McCoy. You're under arrest for the Trail Herd Crew killings."

The following morning at ten A.M. a special session of Kansas Circuit court was convened in Lily's Silver Spur saloon. It was the biggest hall in town. Judge Randolph Pardee brought the court to order and the bailiff read the indictment.

The judge was in town on his usual stop from Topeka, and he had a full docket. Spur's case had been moved to the top of the list.

The judge looked at his cases and peered at the bailiff.

"This is a preliminary hearing then, to ascertain if the defendant is to be held for trial?"

"Yes, Your Honor."

"Then get your paperwork done right next time. Let's get on with it. Who is presenting the case for the state?"

A tall, slender man with a silver-headed cane rose

and nodded to the judge.

"With the permission of the court, I am Dennis Gundarian. I read for the law in Illinois and am the new acting district attorney for the county of Dickinson."

"Proceed, Mr. Gundarian."

"Your Honor, the state will prove that Mr. McCoy rode into town on the train and then did begin to question several persons about the possibility of foul play, stirring up the local people, and spending large amounts of money in gambling and drinking establishments."

"Your Honor, I object," a clear, firm female voice came from the first table behind where Spur was seated.

The judge looked up, his face softened with a smile. It was a momentary lapse.

"Yes, Miss?"

"Your Honor, the defendant seems to have made no provision for counsel for his defense. I offer my services at no cost to the court or the defendant."

"Commendable. And what is your name for the records?"

"Virginia Dale."

"Yes, Miss Dale, your objection?"

"The state has not brought forth a single charge of an illegal act by Mr. McCoy."

The judge looked at Gundarian.

"Your Honor I was laying the groundwork. If I may continue?"

"Please do."

"The state will show that Spur McCoy knew of the

killings of the trail crews before anyone else did, that this foreknowledge indicates a complicity and conspiracy and he was in town to play down any such talk, and to protect the rest of his murderous gang."

"Your Honor," Virginia Dale said, standing quickly. "These are flimsy allegations, unsupported suppositions. Where are the facts in this case?"

Spur turned to look at the woman. She was taller than the average woman, probably five-six. She wore her dark hair pinned back, wore eyeglasses, and held her head high, her shoulders back. She wore a plain black dress with no jewelry.

"Would counsel approach the bench?" the judge said. He studied them carefully. "Mr. Gundarian, these are serious charges, but you seem reluctant to bring forth any solid evidence. Do you have any eyewitness to tie this suspect to the crime? Any physical evidence such as his gun or some object he owns left at the scene?"

"No Your Honor, but he seems like the logical suspect."

"Mr. Gundarian. We may not be formal out here in Kansas, but we do know something of the law. If we dealt with logic we'd be in deep trouble. We are concerned only with facts. Do you have any hard evidence?"

"They said we would have some by now, Your Honor," Gundarian said.

"Your Honor it seems obvious this is a smear attempt by someone," Virginia Dale said. "From what I have discovered about Mr. McCoy's movements in the past two days, he has been doing exactly what I would do if I were a detective sent here to investigate these killings. Since he arrived before they were general knowledge, I deduce that he must have had official alarm that such killings *might* have taken place. I wouldn't rule out the possibility that Mr. McCoy is a private investigator or perhaps a railroad detective. Killing these trail drive crews could mean big trouble for the railroad."

The judge looked at Dennis Gundarian. He held up his hands.

"My people let me down. The evidence we thought we had failed to be produced." He sighed. "It seems I have no course other than to move for a dismissal of all charges."

The judge nodded. "Now there is a logical choice. Return to your places and I'll entertain such a motion."

Ten minutes later Spur and Abby Newland stood outside the Silver Spur bar.

"That was the quickest murder trial in history," she said.

Spur agreed and then moved away quickly to intercept the woman who had helped him. She saw him coming and stopped.

"Miss Dale," he said, "I want to thank you."

"Mr. McCoy, I hope you don't mind my taking up your case. I've been in town for two months and have had not a single case. Most people don't want a woman lawyer."

"Some judges object too, I've heard."

"Yes, but not Judge Pardee."

Abby walked up and smiled at the woman. Spur introduced them.

"You were marvelous," Abby said, meaning it. "What did you say to the judge at that little meeting?"

Virginia Dale told them about it. "They had absolutely no case. I'm going to find out who drew up the complaint. I know it wasn't the sheriff."

"You have an office here?" Spur asked.

She nodded. "Over the general store."

"Thanks, I never know when I might need a lawyer. I'm at the Drover's Cottage. Leave a bill for me there and I'll pay it gladly."

"No, I said there would be no. . . ."

Spur held up his hand. "I pay my obligations. And thank you again. You're a good lawyer, Virginia Dale." She nodded and walked away. Abby caught Spur's arm as they crossed the street toward the hotel.

"She's good," Abby said. "A little plain, but a good lawyer."

"Now, lunch? Jail makes me hungry."

"I thought about you on that hard cot all night. I'll make it up to you tonight."

Over lunch she tried again. "Look, Sweetman Spur. I know you're digging into the killings. Let me help you. There must be some leads here in town I can dig into for you."

He touched her hand, then told her about Ezra Boyce.

"He died not even knowing why. He was living on borrowed time and he didn't know it. Whoever this gang is, it has some kind of an inside man here in town. How else could Ezra be dispatched so quickly? I'm not letting you be exposed to that kind of danger."

She fumbled in her reticule for a moment and then with her handkerchief covering her hand leaned closer to Spur. He felt the round, hard muzzle of a gun in his side.

"Darling Spur, that's a .45 caliber Derringer in your side. It has two barrels and I could blow two big holes through you in two seconds. I told you I've seen a little danger before, remember? I'm a special investigator for the Eastern Division of the Union Pacific Railroad. A railroad detective. Now will you let me help you?"

"First move that man killer," Spur said.

She laughed. "Oh, sure. I really wasn't going to shoot."

He frowned at her.

"And you knew who I was on the train?"

"We do like to know when a U.S. Secret Service man is going on a little trip over our rails. We just weren't sure why, so I volunteered to find out. Glad I did."

Spur frowned. "So all the time on the train and at the hotel, that was all just pretend, just doing your job as a railroad detective. You must have been laughing at me all along. I wondered for a minute why it was so easy, then your great acting job fooled me." He stood up.

"You don't have to act any more, Abby. You can report to your boss that you found out exactly what I was doing."

She stood beside him and whispered. "Spur McCoy, did it look to you like I was acting? Sure, it started out as a lark, a job, but after that first kiss I couldn't hold back if I wanted to. I've never been so excited, so thrilled, so absolutely devastated by a man in my life. You knocked me for a fall. I didn't know what happened. Did I question you a lot? Did I pry into what you were doing? I acted like a damn poor detective if you'll think about it. Now sit down and let's finish our lunch, or I'm going to start screaming and cause a scene."

Spur stood there, thinking about it. No harm had been done. And she hadn't pried into his business. Maybe he shouldn't be quite so angry. Maybe.

He sat down and so did she. "All right, truce for now. I've got a job to do that is more important than our fighting. But we'll settle this later. And now that you mention it there are some things you can do. I have the names of six different herds that could have been sold by the wrong men. But they had to be sold under the right name. Find the buyers who took the cattle, and find out how much was paid for them, and the total number of cattle bought in each herd. I'm trying to work out the pattern these killers are using."

He hesitated. "Have you thought about the money involved? If the killers rustle 15,000 head of cattle at $40 each, that's $600,000. That kind of money can buy a lot of things and a lot of men."

He touched her hand. "Somebody murdered Ezra. Now the same people might have linked me to the investigation, and since you've been seen with me, that touches you as well. What I'm saying is they won't stop now. They have to cover all their tracks. They are going to gun down anybody who is trying to find them. It could get extremely bloody."

"I know how to protect myself," she said, her face sober.

"Have you ever used that Derringer?"

"Yes." Her eyes were steady, serious.

"Have you ever shot at a man?"

"I killed a man in Denver. He had just gunned down my partner on the assignment. He killed two men the day before."

"Then you know how it feels, and you know to be ready." He covered her hand. "Now, if you're still hungry we need to finish our lunch."

CHAPTER 7

SPUR DROPPED ABBY at the hotel and found the upstairs office of Lawyer Virginia Dale. She was in. She quickly put away a sandwich and stood to greet him.

"Mr. McCoy. I have discovered that the complaint against you was issued by a Mr. George Quint. Mr. Quint is a swamper at a saloon in town, a perpetual drunk, a panhandler. He'd sign any paper for a bottle of cheap whiskey."

"Thank you Miss Dale for finding out." He saw that she was uncomfortable. He felt responsible. She had made an attempt to arrange her hair, but she wore the same drab dress.

Spur took two twenty dollar greenbacks from his purse and handed them to her. "I imagine you'll take the paper money our government backs with silver?"

"Oh, yes, of course, it's just as good as gold. But I told you, there was no fee."

"True, Miss Dale, but this is an honorarium. No one can turn down an honorarium." He put the bills on the edge of her desk.

"I will keep in touch, and if I hear of anything having to do with the trail crew killings, I certainly will tell you." She hesitated, looked at the money. "Have you seen the paper bills issued in lieu of coins? Last year the government printed paper in denominations of five cents, ten, twenty, twenty-five and fifty cent bills."

Spur nodded, realizing that she was making conversation, not really wanting the talk to end. "I've seen some of them. Friend of mine says they probably will be withdrawn in another year. People simply don't like paper coins." He stepped closer to her.

"Miss Dale, I'd like to thank you properly for helping me today. Would a kiss on the cheek be in order?"

She blushed, the redness shooting up from her neck to color her face, but she turned and nodded, holding her face up primly. He kissed her cheek, then caught her chin with his hand and turned it. His lips came toward hers gently, slowly, but she didn't turn or lean back. Her eyes closed as his mouth touched hers and he felt her shiver slightly. Then the kiss was over and he stepped back.

"Now, Miss Dale, that was a little more befitting for all the good work you did on my behalf."

She stared at him, her hand reached up to touch her lips, then she sat down suddenly.

"I . . . yes, I agree. Oh, and the money. I can use it. And I thank you . . . I mean. That was nice." She looked up at him and smiled. He nodded, bowed slightly the way he used to in Washington, and walked out of the law office.

He was coming down the wooden steps when a pistol fired ahead of him and to the right, from the mouth of the alley. The hot lead chipped the siding beside his head and Spur pulled the big .44 from his holster. He ran down the last four steps and darted into the alley. A figure slid behind some wooden packing crates ahead of him.

Spur stood for a moment, then jolted to the side against the wall as he saw movement ahead. A hand came out and a six-gun slammed two more rounds his way, but missed. Three rounds.

Spur ran in a quick, short dash twenty feet up the alley to an off-set building, and peered around it from knee height.

Someone ran from an outhouse in the alley ahead and crossed into a saloon. Another man was waiting behind the packing box. Spur started to run again, then faked it and lunged back behind the building. The ambusher fired twice more where Spur would have been.

Five rounds. Nobody in his right mind carried a round under the hammer of a six-gun. The ambusher's weapon was dry. Spur leaped around the building and charged directly at the packing crate.

There was no response for a moment. Then the figure behind the boxes leaped up and ran like a deer down the alley. Spur charged after him, gaining a little by the time they reached the corner. A thin man in brown pants and a denim jacket turned left, away from the main street, only a half block from the raw prairie. Spur gained another ten feet but the fleeing bushwacker was still twenty yards ahead.

Spur saw the man's waiting horse just as he turned and fired a shot behind him. The round went wild. Spur stopped and brought up the Merwin & Hulbert army model .44 and fired twice aiming low. The second heavy slug slammed into the runner's right leg, snapping the bone and tumbling him into the dusty street. His revolver went skittering six feet from his outstretched hand and he screamed in pain as the broken leg bone jammed through the flesh.

Spur ran up toward the bushwacker who writhed in pain. He would still have a hideout. A moment later the man rolled, his right hand filled with a deadly Derringer and it spat once, but missed. Spur shot him through the wrist, then kicked away the small weapon.

Spur came up behind the man, patted him down carefully to be sure he had no other weapon, then nudged the leg twisted at an unnatural angle under the man. The bushwacker screamed.

"Let's do this the easy way," Spur said, the black hole of the .44 centering on the bushwacker's forehead. "I can put one more round through your worthless hide and be done with it." He watched the man's eyes flare in terror.

"Hell, just doing a job."

"Murder is your business?"

"Sometimes, if the money is right."

Spur nudged the broken leg again. The man bit into his lower lip until blood trickled down his chin, but he didn't scream this time.

"Like the trail crews? Seven, eight, nine men in one massacre. That you kind of job?"

"No, not me. I never done that."

"Who hired you to kill me?" Spur asked.

"Don't know."

"I think you do. Half your money before, half after?"

"Yeah, but I don't know who paid. Barkeep dealt me the hand. He said I didn't need to know more than that."

"What barkeep?"

"Lonesome Cowboy. He gave me the cash as he was getting on the eastbound train. He could be anywhere by now."

"So what do I do with you, friend, give you that .44 slug in the head?"

Spur saw two men come out of the back of a store. He yelled at the men. "You two. Get over here and carry this bushwacker to the jail. Sheriff wants to talk to him." The men ran over eagerly, glad to be in on the excitement. Spur sent another man for the town's one doctor and herded his prey to the county jail.

It took Spur a half hour to get the complaint papers filled out, his complaint against the man who was identified as Ike Ernest. When he was locked up, Spur talked with the sheriff, Manfred Zediger, and made it clear he wanted to know anyone who asked about Ernest, or anyone who tried to help him.

"Whoever hired Ernest to bushwack me is still out there and can hire somebody else." The sheriff who was almost six feet tall and heavy, growled agreement, and Spur left knowing he had one lead covered.

Spur still had on his trail dress-up suit when he walked into the Lonesome Cowboy saloon. Business was light. The trail herd crews had thinned out, but more were coming. Spur stood at the bar and waited for the bartender. A short man with an apron around his pot belly and no front teeth walked up and grinned.

"What's for you, friend?"

"Who owns this establishment?"

The apron's eye twitched. "Don't rightly know. Just hired on. Mr. Gundarian, I heard. Manager's over there at that card table."

Spur walked to the table and saw the man stand up suddenly, his hands hovering at his sides over a pair of pearl-handled six-guns.

"Easy, pardner," Spur said, stopping. "Just relax, friend, and take it easy. All I want is some information."

The man's face was still angry, but he controlled it better. His hands fluttered once more, then he crossed his arms over his chest.

"Who the hell are you?"

"McCoy, Spur McCoy, no relation to Joe."

"So?"

"One of your bartenders hired a man to kill me. Just wanted to tell you he didn't finish the job. You want to try?"

The man's attitude changed. He let his hands fall to his sides, twisted them behind him, then shrugged.

"I can't know what the hired help does. I keep the place open, sell booze and keep the killings down to a minimum or the sheriff gets after me. I want no part of no bushwacking."

"Good," Spur said. "Now you tell your boss if he wants to put me under the sod, he'll need a better man than the last one. You savvy?"

The man nodded. Spur stared hard at the saloon man, before turning his back on him and walking out of the establishment. Once outside he moved faster, went into the saloon next door walking rapidly through it to the alley. He found a hiding spot behind a carriage and waited.

Only a minute or two later the small toothless bartender hurried out the back door of the Lonesome Cowboy and walked in the other direction to the street, then six businesses down. Spur ran after him. The small man never looked behind him. He went down the next block a half dozen doors and turned in at the newspaper office.

Spur nodded. At least that tied in. The newsman knew Spur had talked with Ezra. So the newsman had been the trigger on Ezra's death. It tied in. He snapped his fingers and walked back toward the Silver Spur. Kitten might be able to fill him in on something else.

Most of the girls in the saloon seldom worked during the day. Some came in early in the afternoon when a big crowd of trail herd cowboys were in town. It depended how late the girls had worked the night before. Spur found Kitten at a table in the rear of the place sitting alone, drinking a glass of milk.

She scowled at the milk as Spur sat down.

"Lily says it's good for me," she said, nodding at

the glass. "Milk is for babies."

Spur asked her about the newspaperman.

She shrugged. "I've never heard him mentioned. I don't even know his name. How can he be part of it? Maybe as a go between, or a messenger. I don't know. I'll ask Lily."

"No," Spur said sharply. "She must be more deep into this thing that we thought." As they spoke Lily came up, swaying her hips, unbottoning another fastener to let more of her pushed-up breasts show over the low-cut dress.

"Hi, sweetheart. Spur, that lawyer of yours sort of made the county prosecutor look like an idiot today."

"He is an idiot to try a prosecution without evidence."

"Yeah, I agree." Her English accent was much less pronounced. Did she turn it on and off, or was it fake? He wondered.

"Kitten, Phyllis has a message for you. Run along upstairs." She turned to Spur, caught his shoulder, and rubbed against him. "Now I can talk to you alone. First, I really don't want you bothering sweet little Kitten anymore. You upset her and she asks me all sorts of questions. And next, I want you to tell me all about that big bad man who tried to shoot you."

"Everybody in town knows about it by now. What I want you to help me figure out is why he tried?"

"Huh . . . you insulted some cowhand's girl? Or you jostled a cowhand on the boardwalk?"

"Afraid not. It has to be the trail herd killings or my trial. You know anything about that? Is there some tie-in with the killings and anybody here in town?"

He said it casually but watched her closely. Lily never winced or gasped or lifted an eyebrow. She was cool as summer ice.

"Hell, Spur, anything is possible. But what would be the advantage? . . . Oh, the cash from sale of the critters. Yes that could mount up. I'll do some listening for you. All I can promise. Sometimes when you men get feeling real sexed up you say things."

Spur grinned, playing the part. "Yeah, Lily, I remember and we're going to have a rematch one of these days."

"Make it soon, I still got this big hankering to see if you're a real redhead. And there's only one way to know for sure."

They both laughed, and Spur took a step away. "Business first, though, pretty lady. I aim to find out who tried to railroad me on that murder charge and who hired Ernest to take a shot at me. I don't take kindly to either one."

"Can't blame you. But don't get yourself killed finding out. What good would that do?" There was a pleading in her voice and a look in her eyes that he couldn't exactly read. It worried him. Spur grinned and waved.

"See you later, pretty lady," he said, walking out of the saloon into the street under an overcast sky. It looked like a summer lightning storm was brewing. That would make the trail crews unhappy. Lightning and hailstones were the biggest fears of the cowboys.

Spur stood for a minute staring at Abilene. Just an infant town, a little over two years old since the first building went up in 1867. Most of them were still unpainted. Time enough to paint after the boom season of trail drives was over for the year. A few clapboard finished stores, the livery with vertical boards and no paint, and the rails. They made up the town. All but the hotel were one storey with eight foot "false fronts" extending upward to make them look like bigger buildings. One had a complete door jamb and door fitted into the "second storey," of the false front. But the door led directly onto the roof behind the wall.

A cattle boomtown. It would be, if the boom lasted long enough for Abilene to survive these trail herd crew killings. Any rumor could spook drovers to move to a new railroad siding down the line.

Spur walked to the poor excuse for a jail and talked to a deputy. Nobody had been to see the prisoner but the doctor who set his leg and put a cast on it. As Spur had expected, the men who hired him would let the bushwacker sit there and rot since there was no way he could implicate them.

Outside the jail, Spur walked down to the cattle pens, built close to the town, or rather the town grew up around them. There were a couple of thousand bawling, lowing steers and cows in the pens waiting the next string of box cars headed for Chicago. When everything was in smooth working order, Abilene could ship out 120,000 head of cattle a year. The first year in business, 1867, they had moved almost 20,000 head as the pens and equipment got "shook out" late in the season.

Last year they had hit almost 70,000 head and this year the pens had been full most of the time, with a herd or two waiting to be penned from time to time.

Spur found a gaggle of cattle buyers at the Drover's Cottage bar and joined them. Most were from Chicago, some from St. Louis. They were talking about the killings. Spur waited for the chance to ask his question.

"Wouldn't the same crew bringing in three or four herds a season arouse suspicion whoever was buying the critters?"

One of the men who had been doing a lot of talking, shook his cigar. "Hell no. We don't pay that much attention to the crews. The trail boss maybe, but they could rotate the man acting as the trail boss. Now maybe some of the loaders and the cowboys who put the animals in the pens might have seen the same hombre more than once. That's a good possibility."

Back at the cattle pens, Spur made a few inquiries and managed to drum up a conversation with a bearded man in his fifties who wore a beat-up cowboy hat that had one part of the brim torn off and looked as if it had been trampled by dozens of steers.

"My favorite hat," Oliver Farkel said. "Been on two trail drives, and two years here now. You that feller that got let off on them trail herd crew killings?"

"Yep. That's me. You know who laid the trap for me?"

"Not me, son. I just push critters."

"Just the man I'm looking for. You been on the crew here all summer?"

"True."

"Think back. Do you remember seeing any one cowhand on a trail crew that you've seen before, *this summer?*"

"Couldn't be. Takes too long to make a drive to do more than one in a summer. Oh, yeah, I see what kind of a cud you're chawing on. More than once, the same loco cowboy. There was that one-eyed galoot . . . no he was last year, then this year. Hey, they could wear different clothes, beard, no beard. Don't see them often, or very damned long. Just in and out."

He scratched his chin and his fingernails came up filled with dirt. Farkel frowned. "Does seem like there was one guy I swore to the other guys I'd seen before this year, fact not more than two weeks before. They said I'd had too much loco weed in my pipe. Who was that one? A Mex seems to me. Not too tall, moustache. Hey! And that same goddamned *Pinto!* I *knew* I'd seen that pinto before. Not quite as big as a regular quarter horse, but a real sharp cutter. Could tell just where them damned critters were moving before they did. All you had to do was point out the steer and she could cut it out pronto. My God, that was *three* times I seen that Mex on the same Pinto bringing in a herd this summer! Goddamn, you mean to tell me that Mex and the rest of that crew he was with are the mass killers? And they did it more than once, *three* fer Chrisakes *times?*"

Spur calmed him down. "It looks that way. There is a lot more going on here than we know about so far. Don't tell anybody what you just told me. *Nobody*, you understand." Spur told Oliver Farkel about Ezra.

"He was a good kid but he knew too much and somebody killed him. I don't want to have to bury you too, so *don't tell anyone!*"

"Jehosiphats! I'll be goddamned! I'll sure be looking for that little son-of-a-bitch again, I'll tell you, and when I see him, I'm gonna high tail it right to the sheriff's office."

"Good thinking. Now you sit down and try to remember who the other men in that same crew were, and write it down for me. Any names you might have heard as they worked their cattle. I'll be back to see you tomorrow. And Farkel, you keep this quiet, you hear? Then we have a chance to catch them, and you have a much better chance of staying alive."

On the way back to his hotel Spur passed the Silver Spur and he turned in. In spite of what Lily said, he had to talk to Kitten. She was the only impartial ear he had in this town. He wanted to know just how Lily was tied in with the Big Four. Was it possible they were connected with the crew killings? It didn't seem likely, but then $600,000 could buy a lot of loyalty.

He caught a dance hall girl's arm and turned her around. She widened her eyes and put her arms around him, her big breasts spilling half out of her dress as she pressed against him.

"Honey, have I got a surprise for you!" she said.

"I've seen your surprise. Is Kitten here? I have to talk to her."

The girl laughed. "That little baby face won't be hurting my business anymore. Lily 'retired' her. Said she was going to put her somewhere, away from our corrupting influences. I also got the idea she wasn't too pleased about it. She said she couldn't tell a soul where Kitten would be."

Spur let go of the girl and surveyed the big saloon.

Now it was Kitten! They were striking at her because of him! He couldn't let them do that. He had to find Kitten, fast!

CHAPTER 8

LILY WASN'T IN the main part of the saloon. Spur went quickly through the rear velvet curtain and up the steps to her apartment. He didn't bother knocking. When he thrust the door open he found the sitting room vacant.

"Yes?" Lily called from another room.

Spur marched in, his hands on his hips, eyes furious. Lily stood by her bed, she was changing clothes and wore only a thin petticoat. She smiled at Spur and pulled the white cotton slip off and stood before him naked, her firm breasts high and enticing, hips slender and a brown thatch over her crotch.

"Coo, luv. I'm glad you came up. I've been wanting you in the kip all day." Then she noticed his expression and she lifted her brows. "Come on, luv, whatever bothers you we'll talk about after."

Spur nodded and stepped forward, his hands closing around her breasts which were already warm to his touch, pulsating, and quivering. Her naked body pressed against his and her lips searched for his mouth. He kissed her quickly, then pushed her down on the bed and sat beside her.

His hands massaged and petted her breasts, then wandered down her sides, across a little belly and then plunged into the forest of brown thatch.

"Lily, we're going to talk about it right now, or I'm not even taking my pants off."

"You don't have to, just pull it out, Luv."

"Who told you to send Kitten away?"

She frowned. "Nobody. I just figured this was a bad place for her to be."

"I can't accept that, Lily." He bent and nuzzled her breasts, then licked around and around one until he came to her nipple which he kissed softly, then nibbled at it with tender bites.

"Good lord! but that makes me hot. It sets me on fire, Spur. Get undressed, please!"

"Kitten. Who told you to hide her away?"

"Nobody, I told you." Her English accent was entirely gone now.

His hand stroked quickly upward between her parted legs across tender nether lips and she gasped, then moaned. "Spur, come on, don't tease me."

His hand made the trip again, slower this time. She shivered, her whole body shaking for a moment. Spur bent and bit the other nipple, chewing at it, burning a fiery ring of kisses around her tender flesh.

"Christ, Spur, they'd tear my tits off! You don't know how tough they can be."

"Yes I do, I found Ezra Boyce before the sheriff did."

"That boy? The trail crew kid?"

"Yes. Your friends hired someone to slit his throat."

She shivered again, this time from fear. Spur put his hand between her legs, touched her tiny trigger twice, and Lily moaned, and then gave a stifled sob.

"Jesus H. Kerist, they will tear me apart!"

"They never will know how I found out. I guarantee. I'll go out the back door."

"Kerist, Spur!" She grabbed his hand and pushed it between her legs. His finger found the spot again. A dozen times he twanged the node, playing it like a guitar string. She was building. He stopped.

"Spur!"

"The names, now!"

"Oh, God! I can't . . . but I got to! All right, all right! I'll tell you where she is, and you can go get her, and keep her. God, don't let them do what they said they were going to do to her."

"Where?"

"A house, two blocks over, Prairie street they call it this week. Little white house, with green trim and a white picket fence in front. Should be two guns there with her. Oh god, Spur! Now, fuck me now, fuck me good!"

"Yeah soon. First, I get Kitten out of that house, then I owe you one." He reached on the dresser and a moment later pushed something into her hand. "Use that, you won't even know the difference."

Lily looked down and saw an eight-inch-long candle. Spur grinned and headed for the door. As he went into the living room he looked back and Lily was pushing the smooth candle toward her crotch.

He ran down the steps and out the back door. It was still early afternoon. Spur followed the directions and when he was a block away he saw the little house. The town was only a block and a half wide at most places, and there were two blocks this side of the railroad tracks. The house stood by itself with the Kansas prairie extending for miles behind it. No other houses were near. There was no way to sneak up on the place in the daylight.

No ditches, no trees. He stared at the house a moment from a block away and walked rapidly to the General Store. He bought three sticks of dynamite, three fuses and ten feet of fuse that would burn a foot a minute. He made sure he had a packet of stinkers, then went back to the nearest house to the picket fence. It was fifty yards away. He could get into the back yard there and make a throw. If he could throw it out thirty yards, that would be enough.

He studied the house again. It had windows on this side but none on the other. He would make his assault from the windowless side. Spur went to the house and knocked on the front door. A small woman with a baby in her arms answered. He explained that there were some desperados in the next house and he needed to use her back yard for a few minutes. She looked frightened but nodded. Behind the outhouse in the back yard, Spur cut the dynamite fuse. He made one fuse five feet long, and another four feet. He inserted the fuses in the hollow ended dynamite caps, and pushed the solid end of the cap into a hole he gouged in the dynamite. He did the same with all three. There were still three hours to dusk. He couldn't wait. Spur hefted the stick of powder and was counting on it not to explode when it hit. He would throw the first one with the five minute fuse. Then he would do the same thing with the four minute fuse hoping one of them would go off when he wanted it too.

The third he would take with him.

Spur got out his stinkers, broke off one and lit the five minute fuse, hurried to the back of the outhouse and threw the dynamite like a spear as far as he could toward the picket fence. The fuse kept sputtering and trailed out behind like a tail. The dynamite did not explode when it hit the dirt. He lit the second fuse and threw the bomb with similar results.

Then Spur ran back to the street, around the block and came up on the far side of the target. He guessed he had a minute left. This side of the house had no windows.

If he could pretend he was only walking into the prairie, he could get beyond the exposure to the windows in the front of the small, one storey house. If he couldn't, the first explosion should attract the attention of those in the house to the far side.

As he thought about it, the first stick of dynamite exploded with a cracking roar. Spur began running at once, straight forward, then he turned and raced toward the house, his .44 in his right fist and the dynamite stick in the left.

There was no reaction from the house. He heard a door slam, the back one he guessed, and before he heard anything else he had reached the blank wall of the house, panting hard. Spur gasped in lungsful of air, and worked quietly to the rear of the building.

At the far corner he peered around the clapboard, and saw a man standing with hands on both hips staring at the black smudge of smoke still rising from the first explosion. He yelled to someone inside the house. He had a six-gun in his hand, but let it fall to his side. Spur took two quick steps, and smashed the heavy M & H revolver down on the guard's head. The man half turned, his eyes wild, then they rolled up in his head and he fell toward Spur. The agent caught the guard and eased him to the floor, took his six-gun and pushed it in his belt, then looked in the door.

Just then the second stick of dynamite blew. The fuse had burned longer than four minutes. Spur opened the screen door and rushed inside, his revolver cocked and ready.

A man sat at a kitchen table, eating eggs and bacon. A white cloth napkin was tucked in his shirt at his chin and his pistol lay on the table beside him. As he grabbed the weapon Spur shot him through the left eye. The gunman jolted backward in the chair, his knees hitting the table and knocking it over. Spur took the dead man's weapon and ran into the other room. He found Kitten locked in the back bedroom. She was tied hand and foot and stretched out on the bed. The top of her dress had been ripped down exposing her small breasts. Her eyes were wild and a gag covered her mouth.

Spur untied her, talking gently.

"Kitten, I'm here, and I'll take care of you. Nothing to worry about now. The bad men are gone. Don't worry about a thing. Do you understand?" He took the gag off her mouth and Kitten wailed, crying in a sudden rush of tears and blubbering that surprised Spur as he finished untying her. He pulled her dress up to cover her, and went to look for the man outside.

When Spur looked out the back door, he saw that the knocked out guard had recovered and evidently run off. Back inside the small house Spur looked out the front windows. No one had been attracted by the explosions. No one stood in the street. All was deathly still.

Spur went back to Kitten.

"Can you walk?"

"Yes," she blubbered.

"Then ease up on the tears. We need to get away from here, then you can cry all you want to."

She nodded.

"And we won't be taking you back to Lily. You'll stay with a lady friend of mine named Abby."

Kitten nodded and he took her hand, walked quickly past the kitchen to avoid the corpse and out the back door. They walked a quarter of a mile into the prairie, then turned left and went another quarter of a mile and at last came back to the town. No one paid attention as they went in the back door of the Drover's Cottage and up to the second floor.

Spur knocked on Abby's door. She opened it at once.

"It's about time . . ." Abby stopped. "Well, hello."

"Abby, this is Kitten. She's going to be staying with you for a while."

Abby lifted her brows then stepped back as they went inside her room.

Spur explained it quickly.

"So, Kitten, you stay with Abby, and we won't let anybody else know you're here. That means you'll have to eat up here and stay out of sight."

"Really? I'm not a prisoner?"

"Kitten, somebody tried to kill me this morning. They already have killed a boy about eighteen. We think you were next on the list. It's about the trail crew murders, and there is a tremendous amount of money involved. They will stop at nothing to protect the leaders."

"Really kill, dead?" Kitten shivered.

"Right. Abby here is a Southern Pacific Railroad detective. She has a gun and will protect you. But you need to help too, by staying here and being quiet and not answering the door if Abby isn't here. Can you do that?"

Kitten smiled. "To stay alive a girl can do lots of things."

"Good, Kitten. And when this is all over, I'll bet we can get a pass for you on the railroad back to where you came from, or to almost any place you want to go."

"I have an uncle in Chicago."

"Good. Now, Abby. What did you find out about herd size?"

"Those seven names you gave me all turned out to be herds about the same size. One was only 1,000 head, but the other six were from 2,000 to 2,500 head."

Spur nodded. "So they take on only herds that six or seven men usually would be handling. They make their operation look as normal as possible. Three to four days out and 1,000 to 2,500 head. Now we're getting something to work with. We're making progress." He reached over and kissed Abby on the cheek. "That's for a good job. Now, I have one more small mission, then I'll come back and we'll have some supper and get to know one another better. Will that be all right with you, Kitten?"

"Just so I don't have to fuck anybody."

Spur couldn't believe the word coming from the child's lips, but he covered it. "Don't worry, you won't. I'll see you ladies later."

Spur went outside into the softness of dusk, cut past the stores to the alley and came up in back of the Silver Spur saloon. He slipped inside and went directly upstairs to Lily's apartment. The sitting room was empty and unlit but a lamp burned in the bedroom.

Spur moved softly and edged the door open a crack. Lily sat at a small dresser combing her red tinted hair. The lamp flickered as he opened the door and she spoke without turning.

"Come in, Spur, I've been waiting for you."

CHAPTER 9

LILY WAS DRESSED for riding in a split skirt, boots, and a short, soft leather jacket over a white blouse. She turned and smiled at him.

"Spur McCoy, you do have the rest of the evening to spare, don't you?"

"I got Kitten out, she's safe and hidden."

"Good, let's go for a ride." She put on a wide-brimmed hat and tucked her hair inside it. "The horses are in the alley all set and waiting. I'll ride out first and you follow a half block behind. We can't be seen anywhere near each other now, or they're going to know I told you about Kitten."

"Where are we riding?"

"You might be surprised." They went out the back door and he helped her mount the roan. Spur stepped into the saddle on his own rented black from the stable and noticed a blanket roll behind his saddle and a heavy sack of goods. Wherever they were going, they would be prepared.

They rode out of town into the prairie, heading north. After fifteen minutes she stopped and let Spur come alongside. The night was warm, there was no wind blowing, and Spur could hear a pair of night birds calling to each other. He came up beside her so their legs touched and she giggled. He looked over and saw that she had opened the soft jacket and her blouse so her bare breasts showed in the moonlight.

"Help yourself, cowboy," Lily said, pulling his hand up to her chest. "I was gonna wait until we got out there, but riding a fucking horse always did make me horny as hell."

His hands played with her breasts, and she purred in satisfaction. "Hey, are you getting ready?"

"What?"

"Is that pole of yours getting hard?"

"You think a little playing around is going to arouse me?"

"Damn, I hope so. I only tried this once before, but you're man enough to do it."

"What?"

"Hell, make love on horseback."

Spur laughed. "You're joking."

"The hell I am, look."

She flipped the divided skirt back and he saw that it had been buttoned on one side, across the crotch and down the other side. Now it was unbuttoned and she was naked underneath.

"Get it out of your pants, Spur and then I'm going to mount you right there on your saddle. A mid-air transfer."

Spur laughed. "It'll never work."

"Hell it won't, you get it out and ready and I'll show you."

She helped him unbutton his fly and work his stiff lance into the Kansas summer night air. Then she grinned, leaned over, and caught his shoulders. She sat side saddle on her mount for a minute, tied her reins to Spur's saddle thong, and then put her foot in his stirup from the front. A moment later she had swung her other leg over the horse's neck and sat facing him on the black's front shoulders.

"Come on, help me!" she squealed as she laughed, then lifted higher and came closer and reached down to guide his hot blade into her waiting scabbard.

She giggled, almost slipping sideways, then she moaned in surprise and relief . . . and settled gently downward on his lance.

"Goddamn, we made it!" she crooned.

She sat facing him, filled with his rod, holding his shoulders, laughing at him, then kissing him. The black stood still. Spur caught one of her breasts with his free hand and rubbed gently, then she began a strange little motion that surprised and excited him.

"Oh, damn, that is good," she mewed to herself. "So fucking good! It's wild, so great!" She bent forward and kissed Spur, then nibbled at his ear.

"Let's ride, Spur. Get this nag into motion. What would that feel like!"

Spur kicked the black forward and she walked at her normal pace. The effect on the joined bodies was dramatic. The lurching, rolling, forward motion at first made Spur think he was being ripped off at the roots, but it moderated and Lily began bouncing up and down as well.

She was breathing hard, panting now.

"Spur, make her canter, really bounce us! I swear I'm going to explode. Get her moving faster."

Spur did and together the rocking cantering motion doubled and then tripled the pleasure pain of the intercourse and Spur knew he was going to be ruined for life.

"Oh, my god, Spur! I can't stand it, but don't stop!" She shrieked into the stillness of the Kansas night and Spur felt himself explode within her. She collapsed against him, shattered and shivering, vibrating in every cell of her body as a series of climaxes tore through her until she could only moan in exhausted delight. She clung to him as he slowed the black, then stopped her.

It was several minutes before Lily moved. At last she leaned back, laughed and pushed up and away from him, then pulled her mount up and neatly transferred back into her own saddle.

"Well, how do you like the Deluxe Cowboy horseback fuck?"

Spur buttoned his fly and laughed, throwing his head back and letting the sound roll across the dark prairie.

"Lily, you are one hell of a woman. I never even considered doing that. And I don't want you to tell me how you thought of it. It was wild, *wild* that's how it was, and I'm never going to forget those few minutes."

"There's more, cowboy, a *lot* more, we're just getting started, you and me. See that dark swatch of trees up there? There's a little green patch of grass under those trees, fed by a spring which comes from god knows where. If there ain't any squatters there, you and me are going to have a Kansas Moonlight Picnic."

"Now that's another new one."

"Yeah, thought you were a virgin when it come to Kansas Moonlight Picnics. Race you to the grove."

She kicked her mount and the animal raced away. Spur had to try to catch up, and almost made it by the time they came to the woods. The trees were a sudden darkness along a bend in the small stream, now almost dry, but there was a green sward that spread out around a spring that trickled out of a low mound and then vanished into the soft ground on the way to the stream.

They dismounted and Lily busied herself finding sticks and limbs and came back with an armload.

"Can you make a fire, cowboy?"

"You ever see a cowboy who couldn't?" Spur took out his pocket knife, gathered some smaller twigs and limbs, a few bits of dry moss, and backed them up against a small log. He circled them with some stones from the creek. In five minutes he had a good blaze going.

Lily brought the blanket roll and sack of provisions from his saddle, and settled down on the upwind side of the fire. The back log was set to bounce some of the fire's heat toward them to ease the nip that had developed in the air.

Lily laid out a midnight snack of cheese, breads, fruit, and two bottles of wine, a red and a white.

"God, I hope you like wine," she said.

"Can a prairie dog dig a hole?"

She grinned, and poured him a glass half full and

handed it to him. Spur noticed that she had not bothered to put her soft leather jacket back on, and her blouse was open giving room for her breasts to sway into the opening. She had buttoned some of the fasteners around her riding skirt.

Spur wanted her again. She made him feel like a fourteen year old with a constant erection. When she moved one breast popped out of her blouse. Spur moaned and reached and cupped it, caressing it gently.

"I like that, Spur," Lily said. "I want you again, out here in the open, with the stars over us and you on top of me, and we will really make love, soft and gentle."

He felt his stalk rising inside his pants. She brushed it with her hand and smiled.

"Lily, you're amazing, enticing."

She slipped off the blouse and he watched her breasts, with soft red areolas and darker reddish-brown nipples which seemed to enlarge and lift as he stared at them. He bent and kissed one and she smiled.

"Oh, yes, sweetheart, you can do that all night!"

He pulled at her skirt and slid it off. He knew she wore nothing under it but the picture of her lying naked on the blanket in the moonlight and firelight stirred him. She was woman and he was man, male and female. She reached out and helped him undress. When his pants were off she grasped his manhood and crooned to him, then kissed its dark red head and she surged upward, catching him and kissing his lips hard.

He felt a stab of painful need in his groin, and her

fingernails raked up the hardness of his staff and he moaned. Her tongue darted into his mouth, exploring, searching. Their tongues touched, exchanged juices, slid along one another, moved in and out. His breath came in gasps.

"You're so beautiful," she said, her hands rubbing his back, his chest, cradling his manhood and the heavy sack beneath it. "I wish I could see more of you."

"I could built up the fire."

"You move an inch and I'll kill you," she said, bending and kissing the pulsating head of his staff.

Spur tensed and swore under his breath. "You do that once more and I'm liable to erupt all over you." His mouth found her breasts again and he kissed them deliciously, trailing hot, wet kisses and their sides, then attacking the peaks with nibbles, and painting them with saliva with his tongue until they were wet and slick.

Lily moaned, leaned back her head and arched her back, thrusting her throbbing breasts toward him.

They had been sitting beside each other. Now Spur gently pushed her down on her back, his lips descending to her round softly flat belly and worked lower. His hot trail of kisses rushed down her right leg and he felt her part them. He moved to her left and worked up it to the softly scented thatch at her crotch.

She writhed as he worked his way through the lilac forest to the open welcoming pink lips. Her hips rotated slowly, beckoning him. He kissed around it then his lips met her nether lips and she shivered with a quick spasm of release.

"Now, Spur, now. I want you inside!"

His brain screamed with desire, his loins ached with the wanting. She pulled him up from her crotch, spread her legs wider, inviting, urging him.

Spur rested on his hands over her, his bare flesh pressing down on her slender form. Her face was a boiling mass of desire. "Yes, sweetheart, now, do it now!" she shouted.

He lifted and slowly moved toward her. Her hands guided him and then he felt the promised land, the center of the universe, the one true beginning of time and all matter and he thrust forward, plunging into her.

Lily screeched at the joy of it, an animal cry he was sure the other female animals on the prairie understood, the submission, being entered, the ultimate in physical union.

He drove deep, withdrew and she cried out, then he plunged in again and again. She matched his motions with counter thrusts. Their hip bones met with crashing pleasure and agony.

She was building with him, and erupted quickly, only to fill and overflow again, and then a third time as the vibrations jolted him first one way and then another as she kept climaxing again and again.

That triggered his own desire, but it was too fast, it would end too quickly, and he slowed and felt her slow with him and he made it last and last.

She lifted slender legs around his back and clasped them together, pushing herself upward until she hung on him and now her movements were amplified and the freedom gave her a chance to work another deadly-marvelous magic on him.

Passion ruled. There was no time. It stood still. There was no right or wrong: it had melded into one entity—action. There was no tomorrow, the future had ceased; there was only now, no yesterday, no memories, no tomorrow, no dreams, also no responsibility.

There was only now, woman and man and sex and pleasure.

Then it was building again, that heat, that desire, that volcanic presence that once triggered could not be stopped. It came and he groaned, then she shouted and at last he screamed a long primal cry that billowed through the night like a dagger. He exploded into her six powerful times and then fell exhausted in the mini-death and her arms closed around him and pulled him even tighter against her flattened breasts and her heaving sides and she never wanted to let him go.

At once she wanted to talk.

"Spur, I know I'm shameless, but I wanted you from the first instant I saw you. You do that to a girl, you know. Oh, hell, damn right you know! I didn't think it would take me so long, but it's sweeter this way. No, you don't have to say anything. I know you're resting. And I like it this way."

She hugged him tighter. "It's all over town by now, Spur McCoy. Everyone says that you're a detective, probably working for the railroad, or maybe for some Texas cattleman's association. Never heard of one, but they must have some down there. All these crews getting wiped out is bound to cause some problems. Also hear somebody tried to dry-gulch you. Watch your back, Spur, there's more than one gun in town looking to puncture it with a few holes. Not your chest. Word is you can use your iron."

Spur seemed to be asleep, but he was alert and listening to every word.

She reached up and kissed his ear. "Been doing some thinking. The damn Big Four. They put it together, and asked me to sit in as a kind of advisor, weathervane, set of ears. From what they say they are trying to slow down, maybe even stop Joe McCoy and his plans to make Abilene the biggest cattle shipping town in the whole damn country. He's got a good start. We'll push our 120,000 head capacity through town this year."

Spur moved slightly and she smiled.

"Now, just relax, you ain't going anywhere. We got the bottle of wine, and a whole bunch more goodies to eat." He lifted away from her and sat up. She sat beside him.

She leaned over and kissed his lips softly. "Sweet Spur, sweetheart. You ever find anything better than the old crotch box and making love, you let me know."

Spur shook his head, and fed more of the sticks into the glowing embers of the burned down fire.

"Doesn't make sense," Spur said. "Big Four are businessmen, own half the town. The trail herds pour money into this place. Some of the stores take in a thousand dollars a month during the summer. They could close up the rest of the year. Why would they try to discourage the trail herds?"

"I didn't say it would be easy to figure out, luv."

She sliced the cheese, put it on crackers, and poured more wine. There was a length of salami, fruit, cookies, and candies.

"Can you find out what they're trying to do?"

She reached down and touched his wilted shaft.

"Poor baby, I think I killed him."

"Just resting," Spur said. "Can you find out what the Big Four are really up to?"

"Coo, luv. In six months I ain't found out. They don't include me on much."

He reached over and petted her breasts, then kissed both tenderly.

"Lily. Fifty men on seven crews may have died already in this wholesale massacre. And it all happened right here in the area around Abilene. It's a crime that must be cleared up, and the killers hung. If the Big Four have *hired* someone to do this dirty work, they are just as guilty as the men who pull the triggers and throw the knives."

"They don't tell me much."

"You've got to try." His hand slid around her thigh and toward the soft brown pubic hair. "I'll do everything I can to make you happy, if you help me."

"Coo, now there's an offer."

They made love twice more, drank the rest of the wine and went to sleep in each other's arms, one of the blankets over their naked bodies.

Spur woke at dawn, stiff and sore from sleeping on the hard ground. He could still taste the wine. He looked to the south and a little over a mile away he saw a brown sea of cowhide moving slowly toward them. It had to be a herd waiting to get into the loading pens at the railroad.

Spur and Lily got dressed, watered their mounts and headed back to town, taking a route around the upwind side of her herd. Spur guessed there were nearly five thousand animals in the bunch.

He watched Lily riding beside him.

"You will keep your ears open for me, try to find out why the Big Four are trying to discourage herds coming to town?"

She nodded. "I'll try, but they always send me out when the discussion really gets going."

"Just listen, but don't get in trouble with them. I can't prove it, but it looks like whoever is killing the trail crews has some inside contact here in town. Why couldn't it be the Big Four?"

"They aren't killers."

"Take $600,000 and split it five ways, giving one share to the murdering trail crew, and it comes out at more than a $100,000. Do you think each of those four men would turn down a chance to make that much money in one summer?"

"I don't know, Spur. I just don't know."

She smiled at him. "Hey, I do know about last night. That was beautiful, and wonderful and marvelous, and terrific. I've never been better bedded. Never. Tonight I want you to stay in my rooms. I want to examine that great body of yours in strong lamplight for at least six hours. I've got some positions you won't believe. I want to wring you out until you can't even get it hard anymore."

"Twenty times? You sure you can take it?"

"Twenty! Coo. About four, I figure."

They both laughed, parted a half mile from town, and entered the cattle village from opposite ends. He waited until she had tied her horse in back of her saloon, then he went on to the livery.

For the first time in hours he thought of Abby. What was he going to say to her? He shrugged. Why did he have to tell her anything? He had simply been out working on some clues.

Spur touched his hand to his cheek. He hoped Abby couldn't smell any rouge or powder on him. He'd wash up as soon as he got into his room.

CHAPTER 10

HANS KURTZMAN STARED out a second storey window into a new dawn. He was an early riser, always had been. He saw a man dressed in a rumpled brown suit striding along the sidewalk. The movement was supple, alert, rapid with the air of a trained athlete, a runner perhaps, a man ready for anything. The man turned and Kurtzman broke the lighted cigar in half that he had been holding in one hand.

He was staring at Spur McCoy. The detective was still alive. The pair of "experts" he had hired to do the job had bungled it neatly. One dead, the other running for his life on yesterday's eastbound train.

Kurtzman was a large man, on the heavy side, with a full head of black hair and full black beard. Even his eyebrows were shaggy and his arms were hairy. He had come to Abilene to build a hotel, only to find one already up. Damn Joe McCoy! So he had built a modest two-storey, twenty room hotel as a starter, and took in the trail cowboys who wanted a good bed, a bath and some well cooked food before making the return trip. He was making money, but not what he could have if he owned the only hotel. Next time it would be different.

He stared at Spur McCoy's retreating back. Kurtzman wondered again just who hired the tall detective, and why he had come so quickly. There was another month of good drive weather, and some of the herds would crowd the calendar and come in early October.

The trial had been their first mistake. They should have planted the evidence and bribed the witnesses first.

Kurtzman went downstairs to the kitchen, stared at the cook a moment and stepped into the dining room which was not yet open. Five minutes later the cook brought out a platter filled with food he knew Kurtzman wanted: two breakfast steaks, three fried eggs sunnyside up, half a pound of sliced, fried potatoes, six slices of bacon, and a stack of six hotcakes and six patties of sausage. The coffee cup was twice as big as normal and brimming full.

Kurtzman ate quickly, thinking nervously. The others were getting queasy, saying it was time to back off, to try some other plan, perhaps they could spread rumors that Texas Fever had hit some of the herds coming up the trail. That could do the trick in one season. Of course they would have to produce results, some actual Texas fever. He pondered it through breakfast, ordered another cup of coffee and three sweet rolls brought to his office, then walked briskly around the hotel three times before he settled behind his big roll-top desk.

They were committed. There was no chance to turn back now. Kurtzman heard a cough and looked up, startled. He had heard no one come into his office. What he saw made beads of sweat burst out on his forehead. He took two deep breaths and did not move.

Kurtzman was staring at a small man wearing an all-black suit. In each hand he held a six-gun aimed just past Kurtzman's head, one on each side. The man chuckled. There was no humor in the sound. The man's eyes were dull gray. He was clean shaven except for mutton-chop sideburns. His nose was rakish, bent to one side. He wore a black, low-crowned hat that had seen a lot of outdoor thunderstorms and Kansas dust.

The man let the hammers down softly on the weapons' empty chambers and slid them into holsters tied low on his leg.

Hans Kurtzman gave a small sigh of relief. There were one or two men who would love to draw a bead on him. He frowned now and stared hard at he small man.

"How did you get in here?"

"Into your hotel, I came through the front door. Into your office, through the door directly in front of you. I move so no one knows it or sees me. The same way I came into your office. That, Kurtzman is why I am so good at what I do. I understand you're looking for a specialist, an artist with a six-gun."

"I'm afraid Mr. . . ." The small man had not given him a name. "I'm afraid sir, you must have some bad information. I'm a hotel man."

"Some of the time. I also understand you have three partners, and if you say do it, they will go along.

Kurtzman, I know as much about this operation as you do. I don't walk in blind. I've worked in the East for several years, but I decided to move West. I like it here. May go to San Francisco." He paused. "Like I said, I'm a specialist. I make people disappear. They never bother you anymore. It can be done in public, and all messy, or quick and private with a certain mystery attached. I prefer the latter. Can we do business?"

Kurtzman stared at the deadly little man. He knew at once what he was and what he wanted. Word traveled fast in Kurtzman's shadow world.

The hotel man stood, walked to the side of the desk and looked out the window and down the main street.

"I don't know what you're talking about. I could call the sheriff and have you thrown out of my establishment."

"But you won't, because you need me. You've tried twice and both times your men came up beaten: one dead, one wounded and another running as fast as the train would take him. It's time you hired a man who can do the job right."

"And that man would be you?"

"Yes."

"And you guarantee your work?"

"The best guarantee in the world. I accept no payment until the work is finished. If I don't do the job, I don't get paid." The small man spun one of the six-guns. Kurtzman had heard that it could be done without firing a shot but he had never seen anyone manage it. When the spin finished the small man slowed it and the weapon dropped into the holster on the last turn.

"Kurtzman, I've never failed a job yet. If you hire me, you better have the cash money, in gold, no greenbacks. You have the cash ready to go. I move fast."

Kurtzman had already decided he could do business with the small, dangerous man. "Two rules: One, I don't ever want you anywhere near me or this hotel again. Two, you'll get all instructions from the barkeep at the Lonesome Cowboy saloon."

"His name is Zeke," the small man said. "We've met. I told you I know a lot about you and your operation. I must say I'm impressed. Up to this recent problem."

The small man stared coldly at Kurtzman. The hotel man had no doubt that the man could do what he promised.

"We haven't discussed my consultant's fee," the deadly gunman said with a wry smile.

Kurtzman tensed. He did not like the tone of the voice, or the feel of the situation. He had lost control and there was no way to get it back. He felt naked. The man would ask an outrageous price, maybe two hundred dollars.

"My fee will be five hundred dollars, in gold."

Kurtzman gasped and the small man smiled. "You let me know when you're ready. I'd say tonight would be the ideal time."

Kurtzman was still stunned by the size of the payment.

"Five hundred? That's twice what a clerk makes in a year!"

"I am not a clerk, remember that. I am not a cowboy. I am a *specialist*." He moved quickly and the weapon came into his hand as if it were an extention of his arm. The blued, muzzle of the .44 rested against Kurtzman's chest before he could take a step backward. He felt the pressure of the steel barrel and shivered.

But the face behind the weapon was smiling again. Kurtzman heard the hammer released and let down gently, then the weapon moved backward, spun once and nestled in the holster.

"Just a small demonstration, Mr. Kurtzman. You decide you want to do business, I'll be at the Lonesome Cowboy talking with Zeke. If I don't hear from you by three this afternoon, I'll be on the western train."

Kurtzman nodded and when he looked up, the small man and his two guns were gone. Out the door he supposed. The man moved like a lightning flash. There was no question what the Big Four had to do, and it had to be tonight. He would get their approval one at a time, it would be easier that way.

Kurtzman remembered the six-gun pressing against his chest and a chill swept over him. A chill of death. He did not believe in omens. That was rubbish, superstition, ridiculous. This was just another management decision that had to be made and he would make it for all of them. Now he had to back it up, defend it, and pull the queasy along with him. After all, what is one detective more or less?

He checked the gold watch in his vest pocket. Dennis Gundarian would open the Emporium soon. If Kurtzman walked over now he could have some time to talk before Gundarian got busy with his clerks.

Kurtzman had not consulted his partners when he hired the other bushwackers. The money involved was not that large. But this time it had to be a shared fee. He wasn't spending five hundred of his own money.

Hans Kurtzman scowled and walked out to the main desk. He told the clerk where he would be if anything unusual came up. Then Kurtzman headed for the town's biggest and best store and his showdown with Gundarian. This would be the toughest of his partners to convince.

Spur McCoy had barely had time to wash, shave and change into blue jeans and a light plaid shirt, when a knock sounded on his door. It was Abby. She walked in and sat on his made-up bed and looked up at him with a frown.

She started to speak, glanced away and smoothed out the bedspread. Then she smiled at Spur charmingly.

"Well, for a sound sleeper you certainly do make up your own bed early in the day. My bed covers are still a shambles. All tossed and thrown about."

"Yep," Spur said, picked up his gunbelt and strapped it around his waist, then tied down the holster to his leg. He drew the .44 and spun the cylinder. He checked to be sure the cylinders had five loads, then eased the hammer down on the empty one.

"Had breakfast?" he asked.

She shook her head. "I don't think I can eat. I've been worried sick about you all night. I don't think I slept more than fifteen minutes. I see it was all wasted worry." Abby stood and put her fists on her hips. "I can see it was totally wasted. You obviously were in no danger and you are not harmed at all. Our 'ward' is just fine, and she too wonders why you didn't come back last night. You said you had a small job of some kind to do."

"Yep," Spur said, then he grinned. "Thanks for the worry. I just couldn't get done with the job and get back here in time to take you ladies to supper. But I picked up some information. I'm almost certain that the gang doing the killing has inside information and some kind of support right here in town. Now all we have to do is figure out who and why."

"Oh, sure, that's easy. We just go up to every local and ask him if he's a mass murderer." Abby walked around the room glaring at Spur. "You're not going to tell me where you were last night. All right, fine. It's none of my business. I won't ask you. It's just 'Yep' and business as usual." She stopped and sat on the bed. "Now, I've got that out of my system, what are we doing today, and how can I help?"

Spur stepped to her, lifted her gently and kissed her lips. He put his arms around her. Abby held the kiss, wound her arms around his neck and held on. When they broke apart, she purred a soft little tune and leaned her head against his chest.

"Now that is what I call a nice good morning. I don't care near so much what you say now about what we're doing today. In fact, I'm getting more hungry all the time. We can bring something back for Kitten."

Spur held up his hand for quiet. He stared at the door, then grabbed Abby's hand and pulled her toward the wall beside the door. He reached in his luggage and took out a strange looking weapon. It was a double-barreled shotgun with a ten inch barrel and the stock removed and fitted with a curved pistol type grip. He pushed off the safety and aimed the weapon at the door.

Spur had moved quietly to the other side of the door, near the knob and he waited. Abby started to speak but he waved for her to be quiet. They waited. Spur brought the shotgun up again to cover the door.

A knock came almost at once, and Spur's mouth tightened.

"Mr. McCoy? I have a message for you," a man's heavy voice called.

"What? Oh, just a minute," Spur said, cupping one hand around his mouth projecting his voice away from the door.

He made four loud footsteps as if he were walking to the door and on the last one, the door shivered as three lead slugs plowed through the thin wooden panel.

Spur's sawed-off shotgun blasted once, the 12 gauge double ought buck tore through the door as if it were kindling and a scream of rage and agony billowed through the corridor even after the jolting roar of the shotgun faded away. Spur saw Abby put her hands over her ears. He moved silently toward the splintered door and peered through it. A body lay against the far wall of the hall. The man gripped his stomach. Red streams of blood seeped between his fingers which still held a six-gun. Spur opened the door and glanced up and down the hall. Not a face showed. He carried the shotgun with him as he knelt beside the dying man.

"Who paid you?"

The man's pale face turned slightly, his eyes flickered, and tensed. "Perfect plan, shoulda worked," he whispered.

Spur slapped his face easily.

"Who paid you to kill me?"

"Who? You'll never guess." The man's face stiffened, he coughed. His head rolled to one side and he pitched face down on the wooden floor and a long death rattle gushed out.

Spur stared at the dead man for a few seconds. Doors were starting to open down the hall. The Secret Service man caught Abby's hand and they stepped into her room. He told her quickly what to do. She put on her small hat and a shawl and hurried down the steps.

Two minutes later the hotel manager was knocking on Abby's door. Spur opened it and told him precisely what happened. He rented three more rooms on the spot under three different names.

Spur rubbed his jaw, his intense green eyes holding the hotel manager. "This is the third time someone has tried to gun me down. I want it to be the last. If anyone but you and I know where I'm staying in this hotel, I'll come looking for you with my own gun. It's a simple matter of staying alive. Are we clear, you and I, on what I want from you?"

The manager nodded, his bald head bobbing. "Yes,

sir. And I don't blame you a bit. But I will have to charge you for fixing the door."

"I'll pay half the cost, charge the rest to the gent out there in the hall."

Before they finished talking, they saw the sheriff arrive with two deputies. He studied the situation, checked the dead man and had the deputies carry the body down the back stairs.

Spur stood in the hallway waiting.

"Another one, McCoy?"

"He fired first, missed. I was lucky."

"You seem to be lucky a lot lately."

"Better to be lucky than dead, Sheriff."

Abby had told the sheriff what happened. He had made notes on a pad as they walked back to the hotel. The sheriff went over the narrative with Spur who confirmed it.

"Seems like that covers it, McCoy. One more thing. You'll have to pay for the door if the hotel asks, and you'll have to pay for the funeral of this bushwacker if no one claims the body in twenty-four hours."

"Fair enough, Sheriff."

The big man paused. "You are a detective, right. But who do you work for?"

"Is that an official question, Sheriff?"

"Nope, just wondering out loud. This shooting's got to be because of that trial and your digging into the trail crew murders. You find any evidence, you be sure you tell me. Remember, I'm the law in this county."

"Sheriff, you'll be the first help I yell for if I find anything worth an indictment. You can be sure of that."

The big man nodded, tipped his tall brown hat to Abby and walked away down the corridor.

The hotel manager came up the steps and handed Spur an envelope. Inside were three different room keys. Spur took the keys and caught Kitten's hand.

"Moving time," he said. They went to the third floor where Spur set up the ladies in their new room. "Too many people saw you down there," he said. "We don't want anyone to know where you are." Abby nodded. She seemed withdrawn and quiet. She would get over it. Spur told Abby he would be staying in room 324 the rest of the day, and after this would be doing his work at night.

"I can't afford any more holes in my skin, and these guys seem to keep coming after me. I'll make it as hard as I can for them."

Abby smiled. "You have a small nap and I'll be up to see you with some breakfast. It seems I have two recluses now to feed instead of one."

Spur grinned, and told her that he had arranged with the manager for meals in their rooms.

"Now relax," he said. "Abby. There are a few things that need to be done and I'm going to start doing them tonight. I'll tell you about them when I'm through."

CHAPTER 11

A SMALL MAN dressed in black sat at a corner table in the Lonesome Cowboy Saloon nursing a beer. He had heard about the shooting in the Drover's Cottage hotel, and was relieved to hear that some bushwacker was dead and the target, Spur McCoy, was alive and well.

Zeke had raised his eyebrows when word came to the saloon. He looked at the man he knew only as "Guns" and received a blank stare in return. Twice Guns had left the saloon, patroling the street across from the Drover's, looking for McCoy, trying to work out his habit patterns. It was as if the big man had faded into the sunset. Spur hadn't been in the hotel dining room for breakfast or lunch. Now, halfway through the afternoon, Guns was becoming concerned.

You can't kill a man you can't find. The small man took a long pull at the beer and permitted himself a short, satisifed smile. Yes, he had an idea. A little work and it would develop into a plan.

He finished the beer and walked across the street to Drover's Cottage and into the dining room. He would treat himself to the best meal in the place and enjoy a comfortable night's sleep. Tomorrow would be plenty of time to put his plan into effect. He ordered an inch-thick steak and a bottle of wine. By tomorrow night he would have another five hundred dollars in his poke.

Spur spent an hour in Abby and Kitten's new room, talking about Kitten's plans when she got to her uncle's house in Chicago.

"You'll want to go to school, of course," Abby said.

"School, why?" Kitten asked. "I can write my name, read a newspaper, and do ciphers. What more of an education do I need? I ain't never gonna be smart as you Miss Abby, And I don't want to be no railroad detective lady."

Spur smiled and touched her hand. "Kitten, you're fourteen or fifteen now?"

"Fourteen, almost. My birthday is in December." She looked at them and shrugged. "I know, I told you I was fifteen, but that's just what Lily said to tell everyone, since lots of girls get married at fifteen. She said it wouldn't look so bad and she wouldn't get in no trouble."

"She just did," Spur said softly. He would have a long talk with Lily and demand some kind of justice for Kitten. He and Abby talked about the trail crew case. She said the railroad was concerned about it now. She had wired her home office and they had told her to offer any help she could on the murders.

"I need to know more about the 'Big Four' partners," Spur said. "Tonight I start to do some investigations. I'm not sure what I'll find, or if I'll find anything that might help us, but sometimes outlaws save the most incriminating items."

"Let's play poker," Kitten said. "When the girls didn't have any work, we all sat around and played poker. It's no fun unless we play for money, but I don't have any. Would anybody loan me a dollar? I'll pay back."

Spur gave her a wad of paper coins. She had never seen them before and spread the paper nickels, dimes, and quarters out in front of her.

"Two dollars and sixty-five cents," Kitten said. "All right, it's nickel ante and no raise over a dime. Jacks or better to open for five-card draw. Any questions?"

Abby lifted her brows, looked at Spur and nodded. "I know I'm going to lose, but I'll play anyway. Expense account item, I'm sure, but how will I list it?"

They played for an hour and Kitten won almost five dollars after paying back the paper coins to Spur.

"Told you I was good at poker," Kitten said.

A knock sounded on the door. "Your supper," a voice said. "I'll leave it here."

Abby looked at Spur who nodded. He waited two minutes before opening the door and wheeled in a small cart containing supper for three, piping hot and delicious.

Kitten squealed and started opening the covered dishes. Spur remembered he hadn't eaten breakfast or lunch.

Two hours later it was dark outside, and Spur slipped out the back doorway of the Drover's Cottage Hotel. He was dressed in jeans and blue work shirt, his .44, and a low-crowned black hat. He walked around the block and reached the back door of the Emporium, the biggest store in town that bragged it "had everything you need." There were no lights in the first floor. One light showed in a second storey room in the back. Spur settled down to wait and a half hour later the light went out.

He waited another thirty minutes, then tried the back door which was locked. Spur tested the windows. The second one in the back was partly locked with a turning spin catch. He jiggled the window and gradually the thumb-catch worked loose. The window pushed upward without squeaking and he crawled inside.

Spur had been in the store before and knew the office was on the second floor. Once upstairs he found the room. The first thing he did was to get a blanket from downstairs and hang it over the one window, then he lit a lamp and began his search. Gundarian was a man who kept detailed records. There were boxes of them, dating back to the first day he had opened the store almost two years ago. One drawer of files was more recent, detailing stock, orders, workers, profit and loss.

Spur meticulously checked files and drawers and stacks of papers for three hours. He checked his pocket watch. It was nearly midnight. He had carefully put each item back in its place. No one would know he had been there. He checked a shelf of books, and found two on the legal codes of the State of Illinois, another on how to run a business, and one on the best short novels. He moved none of the books. He noticed that all were dust covered on top, except one in the center. It was *Farmer's Better Machinery*. Spur pulled it from the shelf carefully, saw that it had not been used much, no thumb marks or turned-down page corners, no bookmarks. Behind it was a slim four-inch-square notebook bound at the top. Spur took it out and opened it to the first page.

He frowned, turned it to the light and made out the pen and ink writing. "June 14, 1869. J. B. 2,014 head." Spur looked at the entry and felt a sharp jolt of elation. J. B. could stand for Jessie Bodine, one of the names of the owners of stock on the list of seven missing trail herd crews. He turned the page. There was another note: "June 28, 1869. B. K. 3,456 head." Another one? He flipped through the pages. There were six similar entries, the last one made on August 13, 1869, almost two weeks ago. The trail drive entries were about three weeks apart.

Spur sat in the chair near the desk, tapping the small notebook on his knee. Quickly he copied down the notes in the book. There was nothing else, no name, no other data. But there were another twenty or thirty blank pages. Spur started to put the notebook away, then realized it would be the first bit of evidence Gundarian would destroy if he felt threatened. It should stay on the premises. Where to hide it?

Spur looked at the desk. Anywhere inside would be

too obvious. He ran below to the store and, using two matches, found some heavy tape and came back. He took out a lower drawer filled with books and taped the notebook to the underside of the bottom of the drawer. The drawer would still pull out. Gundarian could take the entire office apart searching for the little notebook and hopefully would never think to look for it under a drawer.

Quickly Spur blew out the lamp, took down the blanket he had draped over the window, and placed the blanket back in the stack downstairs. He eased out the window and closed it. With a little luck no one would know that he had been inside the store.

Spur was thoughtful as he walked back toward the hotel. He had one bit of evidence to help hang the big four. Spur took a detour past the Trail's End Hotel. Kurtzman owned it, and it was filled with cowboys taking a few days rest before heading south to Texas. It even had a former Texan clerk to make the trail hands feel at home. He was sure Kurtzman had an office there. But a hotel never sleeps. There would be a night clerk and other workers around the place. It would be impossible for Spur to find the right office and look around without being caught. He would have to pass on Kurtzman.

The other establishment would be even harder to break into, the Abilene Stockman's Bank owned by Nance Victor. There would be no problem in stashing the bloody cash they had produced. The murdering "crew" enjoyed a built-in vault, thanks to the banker-partner.

Spur took the long way back to his hotel, and leaned against the outside of Lily's saloon. He stood in the shadows, but could see the men coming and going through the batwing doors. Two trail drives had finished that day, so an additional twenty to thirty "new" hands were whooping it up in town. One cowboy came storming out of the Silver Spur, fired his six-gun five times into the air, and then sat down in the middle of the dusty street and passed out.

Spur lit a short black cigar and went over the details of the case again. He was in a holding pattern until he could establish enough facts to give him something to go on for another field 'trail' trip. Then he had it! The three week spacing and the size of the herd! That was what he needed, and he had it. They picked off another crew each three weeks. Another one was about due! He stirred, watched a dozen men come out of the Silver Spur and was about ready to return to the hotel when a vaguely familiar figure limped out the door.

Spur watched the man as he came forward. Yes, it had to be, Farkel, the tally man down at the pens. Limp and all, and drunk, blabbering drunk. Spur caught Farkel by the arm as he came abreast and walked him quickly into the alley.

"Thankee, friend. Not sure I can make it." He turned bleary eyed toward Spur. "I know you?"

"You might. Farkel, you're drunk. You been talking?"

"Damn right. I seen them damn killers. I seen them trail herd killers. Know three or four for sure. Damn right. Man got a right to brag a little. Told them in there. Told them all." He stared at Spur in the half light.

"Hey, you're that detective. You got me thinking

about the Mex guy and his goddamned pinto. And I remembered two more of them murdering bastards. One of them talked about Ben, some galoot named Ben works with them, or maybe he's the trail boss."

Oliver Farkel turned and threw up. He rested his arm against the building, put his forehead on the arm and gushed out again losing half of what he had drunk and all of his supper. He came away from the wall wincing and groaning.

There was movement at the front of the alley. They had come only twenty feet into the blackness. Somebody took a step into the narrow gully between buildings. Spur drew his .44.

"Farkel, you old shit, that you in there heaving your guts out?"

Spur stepped away from Farkel so he could silhouette the talker in the lights of the saloon across the street.

"Hell yes, it's me. But I'm half dead. Damned rotgut whiskey."

As the last words left Farkel's mouth Spur saw light glint on metal and a six-gun began blasting from the street. Spur fired at almost the same time, but two solid rounds had been aimed from the other gun before Spur dropped his own hammer. He fired twice more and saw the killer spin and drop out of the light. If Spur had calculated right, the attacker was hit twice. The Secret Service man crawled to where Farkel had been thrown by the force of the big chunks of lead. He found the old-timer face down in the dirt. Spur turned him over gently. He was still alive.

"Big mouth," Farkel said, then he coughed, spitting up blood. His eyes rolled toward Spur. "Should kept my mouth shut," he said. "Yeah, Pinto under a little Mex, and Ben."

"Easy, take it, Farkel. I'll get the doc here and you'll testify yet against those killers."

Farkel shook his head, tried to speak, but a big gout of blood billowed from his mouth and his head slipped to one side. Oliver Farkel would never testify to anything.

Spur lay Farkel down in the alley dust and heard talk at the alley mouth. He stood and walked quietly the long way into the blackness of the alley, vowing that he would put an end to this killing and to the murdering trail crew gang. He had no second thoughts about the man he had shot. If he were dead, good. The bushwacker had charted his course with that risk when he took on the assignment. Spur didn't even want to find out who the assassin was. He had more important things to do.

The first was to get some sleep. He'd done all he could for now. The next stop was to get out on the trail and see if he could find a herd coming along with from 1,500 to 3,000 head. He would check each herd as he moved out, look for the Mex and his pinto and a man named Ben. If he didn't find those elements present in any herd, he would ride until he found the right number of marching longhorns and join the drive crew. He would stop by and tell Abby where he was going, then get some sleep and be on the trail by five in the morning.

CHAPTER 12

ABBY NEWLAND SAW the slap coming but couldn't dodge it. The small man's hand crashed into her face, driving her sideways onto the hotel bed, bringing the taste of blood to her mouth and sudden, angry tears to her eyes.

"Don't!" she shouted. "Leave the girl alone! I'll do whatever you want done, just leave her out of it."

Her summer-wheat-straw hair had tangled over one eye and she brushed it away, scowling at the small man who stood over her. His eyes were dull gray and only mutton-chop sideburns prevented him from being clean shaven. His nose was rakish and bent to one side from some forgotten scuffle. He wore all black. He laughed but there was anger in his voice.

"Miss, I have no intention of harming either of you, if you both do *exactly* what I tell you. First, I want you dressed properly, say for a stroll to the theatre, then perhaps a stop at a fancy restaurant. *Do it now!*" The last three words came as sharp as the lash of a whip and Abby sat up, then stood, touched the corner of her mouth and looked at Kitten. She was smiling, watching the little man with disinterest, a nonchalance that surprised Abby. What must the child have seen in her young life?

"Yes. Yes, we'll be glad to cooperate. I'll need a wrap and for Kitten a shawl. I have one." Abby bustled around getting ready. By then she had forgotten how the man knocked on the door, saying he was bringing dinner, and then burst in with his six-gun ready. He had been sudden and blunt. Abby knew instantly that he was a killer. His eyes gave him away. She would make no attempt for her gun. The intruder who was five feet five would shoot them down in an instant. When they were ready the man nodded.

"Commendable. There may be some manners, some of the finer things, this far West after all. I'll explain *exactly* what I want you to do. You will do what I say or you will die. One of you can die and my plans are still valid. If I must kill both of you, my ploy is ruined, but so are your lovely little bodies, and your *lives.* Think about that before you even *consider* any heroics. Do I communicate with you both adequately?"

"Yes, yes!"

There was a note of panic in Abby's voice, then she controlled it. "Just tell us what to do."

The man watched her a moment, then nodded. "Yes, fear. I expected that. It's a good sign. I don't like to work with people who are unemotional. We will go out the door and down the back stairs to the street. There I have a rig waiting. You both will get in with me and I'll drive. You will make no outcry or any other indication that you are not entirely safe, happy and secure." He caught Abby's face in one hand holding her jaw firmly. "Do you understand me?"

She nodded. He let go.

"I'll be between you. I want you both to hold onto my arms. I have a Derringer in my hand under my coat, and if there is any outcry, the little girl dies first."

Abby shivered.

Ten minutes later they were in a buggy heading out of town. Two saddle horses tied to the rig trotted along behind. Abby had wanted to ask about the horses, but stopped herself. They were still alive, that was enough for now. His plan? He had mentioned his "plan". Then the puzzle cleared and she knew—they were being used as bait, bait to lure Spur into a trap. When the small man had killed Spur from ambush, he would kill both of them as well. The last house drifted by and they were on only a semblance of a road heading north. By then it was too late.

"Where are you taking us?" Abby demanded.

The man started to slap her again but held back. "We're going to the grand ballroom at the Washington Hotel for a Presidential reception." He laughed and again there was mockery in his voice. "Just sit still and keep your mouth shut. You'll find out soon enough."

"You really think you're hot shit, don't you?" Kitten asked, her voice brimming with scorn.

Abby turned in the darkness to look at the girl.

The man guffawed and put his hand on her knee. "Well, that's the little spitfire I heard about, the baby whore who is supposed to be so tight it hurts. We'll have plenty of time to find out about that. Now both of you be quiet."

Kitten's hand crept across the seat and found Abby's and her tight grip told Abby that she was terrified and that the loud talk had been a sham.

An hour later they left the rig. The small man unhitched the buggy horse and put on a halter, riding her bareback. He helped both females mount up. Then he tied the reins to his saddle and led them down a trail that wound along a small stream past some high bluffs. A half hour later they came to a black hole on the side of the cliff.

"Home at last," the man said, swinging down from his horse. He helped both women dismount, then led them up a narrow trail to the blackness. Quickly he lit a pre-set fire located at the front of the cave, then one farther back. He pushed both women inside.

The cave was deep and wide, with a ten-foot ceiling. On one side there lay a double spread of blankets, a small stool and some cooking gear. When the fire brightened, the man found a pair of lanterns and lit them.

"We might as well have some comforts while we wait." He turned to Kitten. "Little Kitten, are you going to run away out there in the dark, when it's scary and where there are lots of night-crawling rattlesnakes and scorpions? Or are you going to sit down and be quiet and be good?"

Kitten shivered. "I don't like snakes, especially rattlesnakes like you, you fucking bastard! But I'll stay inside."

"I like your spunk. You get to be second." He turned and grabbed Abby by the bodice of her dress and tugged her toward him. She resisted, so he put one hand across each breast, dug in his fingers and pulled her to the blankets. He pushed her down, then straddled her.

"I've been waiting for two days to get a look at your tits all bare and swinging free. Do you want to take off your clothes or do I rip them off a piece at a time?"

"I told you, I'll do what you want, just leave Kitten alone." She tried to rise. "You'll have to let me sit up."

He did and watched in the lamplight as she unbuttoned her new blouse. She pulled it over her head and sat there wearing her chemise.

"Keep going," he said, his eyes showing sparks of interest. When she didn't move he ripped the chemise from the neckline to waist and spread it aside. Her big breasts billowed out and he smiled.

"Now that's what I call a nice little bonus for a hard job."

Abby put her arms over her breasts half covering them. He slapped them aside.

"Don't do that. You said you'd do what I wanted. I don't like people to lie to me."

Abby's mind whirled. She had never been hit, nor beaten. The slap in the hotel and the contact now kept her fear level high. She had to think! She couldn't sit here and let him trap Spur. Right? Now she was thinking. But what could she do? Beat him? Get his gun? He kept the six-guns out of her reach as he put one hand on her right breast and caressed it. She thought he would be rough, but he wasn't, more like a lover. Abby felt her breath quicken, saw her nipples begin to rise although she was screaming at her body not to react.

Without noticing it happen, she realized that his hand was under her skirt and had thrust up between her legs almost to her crotch. She trembled.

"What's the matter, pretty lady with the big tits? Don't you think I'm man enough to satisfy you? Worried about how it's going to be with me? Don't fret, I'll give you one of the best fucks you can remember."

He had pulled his hands from under her skirt, and quickly unbuttoned the side and pushed the skirt down, along with her three petticoats. He laughed at her underdrawers. They were her best ones with fancy lace and pink bows. Roughly he jerked them down and over her feet.

Naked. Abby had been naked before and with men before, but never with someone like this. She knew he was a killer. He would murder them when they had served their purpose. *What could she do?*

Through the dim lantern light she glanced around the cave. There were no weapons, no tools, just the small fire and two lanterns. She could break one of the lanterns over his head and douse him with burning coal oil. The lantern probably would not break and she would only put it out.

Get his gun!

The idea came again and she watched him. His hands found her breasts and she leaned forward so her big orbs swung out and seemed larger.

"Oh, damn but they are nice ones!" the man said, pulling at her breasts, roughly petting them. His pistol handles gleamed on his thighs, but they were too far away. She moved and touched his fly, then worked her hand lower.

The man laughed, knowingly. "Yeah, little bitch, you go ahead, play with him, he's damn ready."

She reached lower to his crotch and was ready to surge across him and jerk one of the guns from his holster when he turned and pushed backward, away from her, then grabbing her hanging breasts he pulled them down so he could lie on his back and nibble at her nipples.

For a fleeting moment, Abby hoped that she could tease him, excite him, cool him off and make it all last long enough so that Spur would find the note she had seen the man leave and come for them. First she had to disable this killer or at least stall him until Spur could catch him with his pants around his ankles, or better yet, as naked as she was.

She reached down and unbuttoned his shirt and he grinned upward, sucking as much of one breast into his mouth as he could. She knew her body was responding, felt a wetness at her crotch, but denied it and tried to figure how to strike back.

"Take your shirt off. I like men all bare."

He bit her breast but she didn't cry out. He backed away from her and snorted.

"Little lady. Or maybe I should say big-titted lady, I don't care what you like. I'm the one giving orders. You take them and do what you're told. I never take off my pants, my boots or my six guns. You touch either weapon and you're dead in about a second and a half. You understand?"

She nodded.

He sat up and pushed her flat on her back so quickly she felt the whole cave spinning around, then gradually it stopped and she blinked.

"Good, just so we understand each other. Now stay there." He peeled off his shirt and threw it to Kitten who sat beside the second lantern.

"Learning anything, little whore? Want to give big tits here any advice about how you fucked all those cowboys?"

"Stop it! You don't have to be so. . . ."

He slapped Abby with the back of his hand, bringing a spot of blood to the corner of her mouth. Abby choked back a cry and sniffled as her eyes misted. She wanted to cry, but she couldn't. It would only give him more pleasure. She had to slow him down.

"The little whore is holding up a lot better than you are with your big pillows. Now be quiet and don't move." He ran to the front of the cave in the darkness. Kitten shrugged when Abby looked at her.

"Don't fight him," Kitten whispered. "It doesn't hurt so much that way, I know."

He returned quickly, grinning, holstering his big .44's and kneeling between Abby's legs. He stretched them wide and his hand found her tender spot.

"Hey, yes, she's all wet and ready. I figure there's no rush, we've got two, maybe three hours to play." As he talked his hand rubbed around and around on her mound and over her heartland, back up her tender, sensitive inner thighs and then cupped her womanhood.

"That feel good, little woman? You like that? You want to get petted and poked a little more?"

He moved the lantern so he could see her better, then his finger found the hard node above her tender throbbing nether lips and he stoked it twice.

Abby moaned, not able to stop. For the moment she forgot about everything but the mysterious, mind-numbing surge of powerful emotion that those two strokes had produced. She felt her whole body quivering with the thrill of it. Right then she knew that there was only one thing she wanted, this man's sex. She forgot where she was, forgot who the man was, wanting only one more touch of that marvelous finger!

"Damn your balls!" a thin, young voice screamed.

Abby jolted open her eyes and in a montage of wild action saw Kitten swinging the lantern by the metal handle. The first attack with the weapon sent the lantern bouncing off the man's shoulder. Kitten jumped forward and swung the lantern with both hands. The killer barely had time to throw up his hands to keep the solid base of the lantern from smashing into his head.

He roared with pain and rage as he surged to his feet, darting one way, then the other. He caught the next wild swing of the lantern and twisted it from Kitten's hands.

He slapped her half a dozen times until she slid to the floor. It took him only a moment to strip her and tie her hands and feet. Then he carried her outside and came back without her. He looked at Abby and shook his head.

"What a damn waste of time! We could be pounding away at it by now. Instead I've got that brat fighting with me." He stood over Abby.

"She's very young," Abby said. "She doesn't understand."

"Christ, woman. She understands, probably better than you do. And she knows what's coming." He knelt between Abby's thighs and stared at her luscious, ready body. He sighed and stood.

"Goddamnit!" the man said softly. "There is nothing I would rather do than spend the next three or four hours with that glorious body of yours." He buttoned up the fly of his pants. "However, business first. After my work is done, I'll come back and the three of us will enjoy each other all night."

He bent down and brought Abby's legs together to tie them. He tied her hands and left her on the blankets. He walked to the front of the cave where Kitten was tied to a post driven into the ground. She was outside the cave but under an overhang of rock. The fire from inside left her in shadows.

The small man stood in front of her, his hand caressing Kitten's young, still forming breast. "You're going to be a beauty when you grow up and fill out. That is if you do grow up. Little Darling, you stay right there. I have some business to attend to, then when I come back we'll investigate a three-way game on the blanket. It should be amusing, don't you think?"

Kitten spat at him, hitting his shirt.

"Fire, I like a little fire in my women, and my girls. Are you really as tight as everyone says?"

"Your little nub wouldn't be tight in a thimble, you asshole," Kitten flashed back at him.

"You save some of that fire, I'll blow you out later." The deadly little man chuckled as he ran down the ramp to the stream bed where he had left the horses. He hid two of them on up the canyon in the brush and rode the best one back past the cave and downstream. He rode for fifteen minutes, then put the horse in another patch of brush near the stream, and checked out the narrow place in the gully they had just traveled.

It looked as good in the moonlight as he remembered. The spot was six feet wide which any rider coming upstream would have to pass through. It set up a perfect ambush location. He found rocks fifteen feet away where he could hide.

Next he laid out both of his six-guns and checked the action, and the loads. When he was satisfied that both had six rounds and were ready to go, he sat down behind the rocks and waited.

For a moment he thought he had miscalculated. No, it would take Spur at least an hour, maybe two, to ride up here after he found the note. The man would ask no help, he would come straight here to rescue his friends. And that meant his death.

From fifteen feet away there was no chance that the target could get away. It was a simple shot, and he had twelve rounds waiting to go.

The man dressed all in black looked at the moon and the stars. The big dipper was high in the sky, it couldn't even be nine. He might have a long wait.

Spur would probably be up half the night talking and questioning people. Spur seemed to work day and night. But his working days were about over.

An hour later the small man thought he heard hoofbeats, but it turned out to be the wings of an owl churning the air. He became fully alert. His mind drifted back to his beginnings. He did not start out to be a professional exterminator. It happened. He had been a schoolmaster in an eastern private academy. Twice he was insulted and once manhandled by a student's irate father. When the next testy situation occurred he had drawn a pistol and challenged the bully to a fair fight. In the duel he killed the big man with one shot through the heart.

He was immediately discharged from the school, and when the police came looking for him he moved West. Everywhere he went there was someone who would hire him for a small task. At first he worked as a bodyguard, then running someone off some land, and gradually he went into the "disappearing" trade which was popular with a number of people, including attractive women and a town council or two.

He watched a night owl sweep down and land on a mouse that thought the darkness would protect it. The darkness was no protection for anyone.

But it was convenient. He preferred to work at night. That way a man didn't have to see the expression on the victim as he died.

Far down the little valley came sounds of a horse. This time it *was* hoofbeats. He picked up his guns and leveled both across the top of the rock. He would be ready. Within a few minutes Spur McCoy would die.

CHAPTER 13

SPUR STOPPED by his first room in the Drover's Cottage and found the door repaired and varnished. His key worked but no one was there. No one was next door either. He went up to room 324 and put together a small bag of essentials, including the chopped-off shotgun, a box of shells and more rounds for his .44. He also took a jacket and a change of pants. Spur went down the hall to Abby's room and knocked. There was no response. He knocked again, then used his key and tip-toed inside. A light burned low on the dresser. No one was there. The chair was tipped over, the bed covers were scattered on the floor. He saw the note under the lamp and ran to it.

It was written on plain paper with a pencil:

> "Spur McCoy. You're a hard man to find. But I decided the best way was to have you come find me. Both ladies are with me. I figure you'll want to come make sure they are safe and not be-

ing taken advantage of. I must say Abby is a delicious looking woman, and I intend to see just how delicious she is long before you'll be able to find us. No, we're not in town. Matter of fact our accommodations are rather primitive. It's a cave five miles north of town near a point called Twin Bluffs. I'm sure you'll be able to find it. Yes, I'll be ready for you when you come. Both Abby and little Kitten say hello. Now, I have to do. I'm getting anxious to chew on Abby's big breasts. Hurry, I'll be waiting."

Spur stared at the note. He read it again. This was another assassin, but a smart one. He was a professional and would be a real challenge. There was no question that Spur would not pick up the gauntlet. That was assumed, and the kidnapper knew it. Unfortunately the man had picked the place for the confrontation. At least Spur could pick the time. The problem was the longer he waited, the more jeopardy he was creating for both Abby and Kitten.

He would not panic. Planning was wiser. Just like a military campaign. Surprise was always a good element. He went back to his room, threw in more rounds for the .44 and carried the small, cloth carpet bag down the steps.

Five minutes later he showed the note to Sheriff Jurgens.

"He wants me, he's a professional, a hired killer, and from what I see here, he's a top man in his field."

The sheriff agreed. "I can get a posse in the morning."

"No good, Sheriff. He could have raped and killed

them both by morning. This is a clever, intelligent professional killer out there. He'll be expecting me to high tail it right out the trail north for those bluffs. He'll expect me to come alone, and I will, but you'll be cutting across country. Only that isn't the way it will work.

"We're about the same size. You wear my hat and ride my black, and head for the bluffs. I'll be moving as fast as two horses will take me cross country. How far are the bluffs?

"Five miles."

"Good. I'll take two horses and pound them hard at full gallop all the way. And I want a fine rifle, something with some reach and accuracy."

"It's a trap to bushwack you again, McCoy."

"I know, that's what I get paid for. Now are you with me, or do I go alone?"

The sheriff went to the gun case and took off the padlock.

"McCoy, you don't know where the bluffs are. I've got to go too. He doesn't want you to get to the bluffs. He'll try to take you out a half mile or so this side. There's a narrow place in the trail where it goes along a little stream. Shortest way to get to the bluff is right through there."

Spur considered it. "Let's ride and plan it out as we go. I'm ready."

They were on the trail north five minutes later.

"He's mine," Spur said. "If he doesn't take me out, he's mine, and if he hurts either of those women, he won't go fast."

"Who are you, McCoy?"

"I've got credentials, Sheriff. I'll show you when this is all over."

Sheriff Jurgens watched Spur carefully as they rode. "So far I've got no reason to doubt your word, McCoy. I've seen enough men to sort the good ones from the rotten kind. I'll back your play. But one change. I'm the one who rides through that bottleneck down there on the river. In this county, I'm paid to get shot at. We'll set it up. You can ride hard, get ahead of me, get on top and be waiting. You light a match when you're set on top, then I'll ride through. You see any gunplay below, you blast hard and fast with that carbine. If we can nail him there it will be best."

They hit the stream twenty minutes later and slowed their mounts. It was nearly one-thirty A.M.

"Now, McCoy, this is my country. You bear left here and you'll be climbing a gentle rise with the stream below you. Just keep going. After a half a mile you'll come to a stand of cottonwood along the creek. There a little stream cuts through the false bluffs and it's a real bottleneck. That's where the killer should make his play. If he doesn't we'll go on together. You can ride back to the creek a quarter of a mile farther down. The bluffs and the cave are another half mile straight ahead, upstream. You'll see the bluffs and the cave is about twenty feet above the stream. Can't miss it. If we get that far we should come in one from each side."

They changed horses and hats, and Spur checked the Spencer repeating rifle. He had used it before. It was a carbine, only 43 inches long, and could fire seven shots as fast as a man could work the trigger guard lever and cock the hammer. The .56 caliber round was a little low on stopping power but at short range it could tear a hole a mile wide in a man.

Spur had his chopped shotgun, his .44 and the Spencer. He took another dozen Spencer rounds, waved at the sheriff and moved up the slight rise that lay ahead of him.

Ten minutes later he was above the stream, but still not more than two hundred feet. For Kansas it was a mountain. He saw the sheriff moving along the flat creekbed below, going slowly, obstensibly watching his flanks. Spur moved his horse slowly to cut down on the noise. When he felt he was nearing the top of the rise, he got off, tethered his horse and ran quietly the last twenty yards to the crest. On the other side was a reverse slope much like the one he had just come up. He slid over the skyline position and stared down the cutbank at the trickle of water below. He could see the entrance, the cut through the bluff. It was no more than fifteen feet wide and a rider would have to splash through part of the stream to get around the jutting hard shale that had not washed away with the soft clay and dirt as the river cut the path.

Spur stared into the surrounding jumble of rocks and shale in front of the opening, but could not spot anyone hiding. He listened now, but heard only the gentle sigh of a night breeze, and some birds. A coyote howled once and Spur knew it was the real thing. He wished he had cat eyes so he could see in the dark. Spur crawled back over the crest and lit two stinker matches and waved them. Then went back and found a good spot and lay down silently, making sure a round was in the Spencer's chamber and quietly cocked the heavy hammer.

Then he waited.

He heard a horse coming before he saw it. The plan had been for the sheriff to ride through hard and fast, hoping to throw off any aim of a bushwhacker if he were there. Now the plan seemed too dangerous. Spur had no idea the distances would be so short. The gunman would have nearly a point blank shot if he took it at the right time. Spur guessed where the killer might be, and sighted in on the rocks. He would need no elevation, and there was no wind. He had seven shots. One of them had to find the mark. Spur would have muzzle flashes to guide his rounds. He would fire above them, and pattern the area.

It was the best he could hope for.

The sound of the horse hoofs had quieted for a moment. It was according to plan. The rider would see the "gate"—know it was a danger spot and slow, then with determination, charge on through.

Below in the pale moonlight Spur watched the drama unfold.

First there was nothing, then hoofbeats pounding on rocks and a flash of black jolted through the opening. Spur watched, saw a muzzle flash and heard a report. The rider was past, and Spur had triggered a round at the flash, worked the lever and the cocking hammer and slammed more lead at the bushwhacker. He repeated the message five more times, but saw no more flashes from below.

Then Spur found his mount and rode as fast as he could down the slope, cut down the steep sides of the cliff as soon as he could do it safely, and rode back toward the bottleneck. Fifty yards from the bluff opening he found his black. Sheriff Jurgens slumped in the saddle holding his left shoulder.

"Bastard winged me," the sheriff said. "I heard something go past me the other side of the stream. Must have been a horse, and it had to be the gunman. He would have come in and finished me off it you hadn't made it hot for him with that Spencer."

"Let's look at that shoulder," Spur said.

The sheriff waved him off. "Don't bother. You get on ahead. Take the far side of the cave, and I'll come up on this side."

The sheriff slumped to the saddle and almost fell. Spur swung down, caught the sheriff by his good arm and helped him down from the leather.

"Pardner, you can't ride anywhere. You sit here and I'll take care of the business up ahead and be back for you. One of those seven Spencer rounds must have caught some of our killer's flesh. I'll go in and clean up and be right back." Spur took his black, tied the sheriff's mount to a bush and made sure the lawman was comfortable, then he stepped into the saddle and rode hard up the trail toward the bluffs ahead and the cave.

He had no idea what to expect when he came close to the cave. Spur stopped his black a quarter of a mile away, tied her to a tree and ran silently the rest of the way. He carried the carbine with a full tube of seven rounds, his six-gun in the holster and the chopped shotgun pushed under the heavy gun belt at his left side. He had a pocket full of shotgun shells.

The small gully widened for a while, then narrowed again, and Spur saw the bluffs rising higher on each side. Soon it was little more than a twenty-foot wide cut as the small stream wound through the towering bluffs.

Spur saw the blackness ahead and to the left, across the small stream. He wondered what kind of a reception he would get: a blast of six-guns, a knife, a noose, maybe a call before a point blank shot. He wasn't walking into anything. He lay in the darkness and watched the blackness of the hole. Once he saw a dark figure move across the entrance, then vanish.

So, his assassin was in and moving. He must not have been wounded badly if he were hit at all. Too bad.

Spur wondered about working up closer. He wished he had a bow and arrow to fire flaming arrows into the cave to give some light.

As he thought it a fire sprung up in front of the cave producing a glowing brightness revealing the front of the bluff and the cavern behind it. To Spur's surprise he saw Abby pushed into the light. She was naked, her hands bound behind her. Something was on her chest. Spur looked closer and saw that it was a six-gun with a string attached to the trigger. The muzzle was just below her chin. A few seconds later Kitten was pushed into the light. She too was naked, her slender figure looking boyish except for her small round breasts. Another pistol was tied to her chest with the muzzle only an inch from her chin.

A voice bounced from the walls of the cavern in a long, mocking laugh. Spur frowned trying to pin down the location. At last he decided it had to be coming from near the cavern.

"Spur, you must be out there somewhere by now, laying in the darkness, trying to figure out what to do. Don't bother. There is nothing you can do to help these beautiful, naked ladies. I've already sampled their delightful bodies. They are perfection. But then you already know that."

The man laughed and the sound bounced around the darkened cliffs. "Notice how tightly the strings are attached to the triggers, Spur McCoy. The slightest motion by either of the beauties could snap off a shot. And you know that neither lady could live through a shot like that. If you try to rescue them, you damn well may kill them. So, down to cases. We're both men of the world. We can compromise. I'll take back your badge, your hat and horse and your cut-down shotgun and prove that I killed you. You get the satisfaction of knowing that I'll let the women go without any more harm. It's an even trade, your worthless life for theirs. Interested?"

"I'll see you in hell first," Spur shouted.

At once a rattling, snarling sound of rifle fire exploded in the confined space, and hot lead sprayed the spot where Spur lay. He dove behind a large rock and heard the bullets flying just over and around him.

A Gatling gun was firing: the 10-barrel, crank revolved weapn that could fire 400 rounds a minute, if the black powder didn't foul the breach. Spur had no idea what the madman had mounted the Gatling on.

Usually the army used a horse-drawn two-wheel cassion. The cranking rotated the barrels that were fed rounds one at a time and fired automatically as fast as the operator could turn the crank. The firing eased off and Spur lay there helpless. He couldn't shoot back without the risk of hitting the women. Nor could he advance into such a hail of fire.

The moment the Gatling gun stopped shooting he looked at the mouth of the cave again. The gun had been set up just below, and had to be protected by some kind of rock fortress with a shooting slot, built of blocks of stone.

Military tactics. He would have to take another approach. Spur stared over the rock at the cave, then upward. There was a slight overhang above it and then the top of the bluff about fifty feet above. He figured the Gatling gun was set up beyond the overhang.

His mind made up, Spur moved with great quietness and caution until he was away from the site. He found the black where he had left her and checked, yes, the length of rope he had tied to the saddle was still there. Still not sure exactly what he would do, Spur searched the face of the bluff for a way up. He found one another hundred yards along, and worked up the narrow break on foot, climbing quickly and surely until he was on top. Then he eased along the sharp drop off until he recognized the turn in the stream below and figured exactly where the cave was.

Spur bellied up to the very edge of the cliff and looked down. He could not see the cave entrance, but there was a flat place in front of it that had been piled with rocks to build up a fort. The Gating gun was mounted with its barrels poking through the make-shift wall. Spur found rocks on top a short way back from the drop-off. He carred a dozen fifty pound chunks of rock to the edge, then went for three more. He judged the distance, and the chance of hitting the chatter gun below.

Yes, it was worth the risk. It would give away his position, but it also would take away a heavy weapon against him.

Spur picked the second largest rock and placed the largest beside it on the edge. He couldn't roll the rocks, they would leap away from the cliff face and slant outward when they hit the overhang. He had to toss them so they just cleared the overhang and hit on the patio below.

Spur checked his watch. Two-thirty. Another three hours to dawn. He worked faster, bringing up all the heavy rocks, then lifting the first one and judging the distance. He tossed the forty pound rock with both hands, saw it sail downward, hit the overhang, shatter, and fall harmlessly well in front of the target. He at once threw the next boulder, then another and another. Then he looked to see if they hit anything. He watched the path of the next heavy rock. It soared outward, then fell quickly slipping past the overhang and smashing directly on top of the Gatling gun. The round barrel with its ten shooting chambers was bent and twisted beyond use.

Spur heard a scream of anger from below, and had a momentary glimpse of the kidnapper who edged out from the overhang for a quick look, then darted back to safety.

Spur threw the rest of the rocks, then ran back to his access and worked down the face of the incline to the stream bed below. He moved up with more confidence, working his way slowly, quietly.

He didn't move a leaf, break a twig, or bend a branch. He stayed close to the cliff wall where a friendly moon shadow gave him some protection against being spotted. As he moved toward the opening he heard the hired killer screaming. Spur ignored the jibes, the threats. The women would do the killer no good dead. They were the bait in the trap.

Spur edged slowly around a boulder and stared at the entrance to the cave. He had come to within fifty feet of it, and saw that the fire had burned down to only a glow, but it still gave off enough light to see that the two women were still tied. Both looked cold in their naked plight.

He edged closer, then stopped when a shot blazed into the night from the cave mouth. The round had been aimed across the stream at shadows on the other side. Good, the killer was getting nervous. Spur would not let him know where he was. Another shot smashed into the quietness of the Kansas night, but seemed to be aimed in the other direction.

Spur wormed forward, now crawling on his hands and knees, the cut-down shotgun still in his belt, the carbine pulled along by the barrel in one hand, the butt trailing in the dirt. He made another ten feet and rested. There were a few boulders between him and the slight incline leading to the cave entrance. If the killer didn't glance in his direction, Spur might be able to surprise the man. Spur parked the carbine against the wall. It had served its purpose. He brought the short shotgun around and checked the safety, then worked silently forward.

In the shadows behind the fire, in the blackness six feet inside the cave mouth, Guns lay waiting. He had his bait out, the victim was out there somewhere, and sooner or later he would come and try to rescue the two women. They always did. It was a formula that had worked time and time again. And right now he had the patience to wait out Spur McCoy.

Too bad about the Gatling. He had stolen it from an army unit a month ago and packed it around in a big box. At least he had some use from it. Who would have guessed McCoy would throw rocks?

Guns stared into the blackness. He didn't have to catch McCoy sneaking up. Just wait until the man showed himself in the glow of the fire and pump six slugs into his form.

Easy.

But the longer the hired killer waited, the harder it seemed to get. Why wasn't the big man making his move? Why didn't he charge in to save the women? Was he strange? Why didn't he act the way other men had? Guns ground his teeth together for a minute, then tried to relax. It couldn't be much longer. One of the women was crying. That ought to whip McCoy into action. Spur would come closer and get in range.

Guns wished he could see more from his hiding spot. He could only watch half the flat place in front of the cave, including the junk that had been a working Gatling gun. He could see the low wall and the right hand edge where the women were tied.

A soft wind had sprung up. It bothered Guns, but he could still hear everything that went on in front of the cave. He reassured himself. Another five minutes and McCoy would come smoking out of the darkness, his six-gun blasting into the cave entrance as he hoped to get in a lucky shot. Then McCoy would go down the way all the others had, quick and clean. He wondered who the second man with the rifle on the bluff had been.

By rights Guns knew he should have killed McCoy at the narrow place. But the rifle from above had prevented him from getting off a second killing shot when the figure had been scarcely ten feet away. He simply couldn't miss a man at ten feet. But if you can't shoot you can't hit. The rifle had been so accurate it had driven Guns low behind the rock during the exact few seconds when he should have been shooting.

No matter, it would be over soon. Then he would untie the women, enjoy them both and leave them in the cave. He would leave a note in town telling where they were, and they would be found, but long after he was aboard the westbound train. Spur McCoy's body would never be found. He smiled and waited.

Outside the cave, Spur worked up slowly. No Indian could have done it better. He had been patient, careful, and skillful in moving up on the entrance. He knew that any click of metal, any jangle of coins, any thud of boot on rock would bring a hail of hot lead death.

Spur carried the shotgun aimed ahead all the time, with one finger on the trigger. He would not fire if it would endanger the women. But if all went well, in another ten feet he would be to the edge of the cave mouth. He had reached the edge of the flat place in front of the cave.

The fire was a dull red glow, but still cast a flickering shadow as it flamed up now and then burning into a foot thick log. Spur could see both women standing where he had first noticed them, worried he was sure, and half paralyzed with fear. He guessed they had been tied in place by their feet. There was no way he could cross the open space of the cave entrance to get to them now.

Where was the enemy? Spur decided he must be in or near the cave entrance, kneeling, waiting for Spur to show himself. Then a quick series of shots and it would be over. Spur looked at the scatter gun in his hand. With the barrels cut off so short, the shot would flare out from the muzzle at once, and fifteen feet ahead it would splatter into an area six feet wide. Two quick rounds from the shotgun should cover the whole twelve feet of the cave mouth. The first to the left, then the second barrel to the right. The double ought buckshot was the size of .38 slugs, twelve of them crammed into the long shotgun rounds. He had them specially made. His little shotgun was no weapon to go up against, ever.

Spur thought it through again. He was as close as he could get and maintain any surprise. Any closer and the spread of the pattern might be too narrow. This was the time.

Spur pushed off the shotgun safety and knelt, held the shotgun to his shoulder and covered the left side of the tunnel. He leaped out three feet and fired at once, the blast ripping the starlit Kansas night into a million shards of splattering lead, screaming richochets and billowing concussions of overlapping sounds.

Spur pulled the trigger again, moving the barrel a scant six inches to the right to cover the rest of the cave. The second explosion of the shotgun came surging in over the remainder of the first and the sounds comingled and enveloped the whole area in a baleful series of echoing reverberations.

When the sound echoed into extinction, Spur could hear a woman crying softly. He heard a moan from the cave entrance, and started to lift up, but a .44 slug parted the air a foot from his skull and he fell back to the dirt.

"Not bad, detective," a tight voice said from the darkness inside the cave. "But I'm not dead yet. You will be though when you come to get me. I still hold all the aces."

"You're hit, wounded bad. I can tell. I've heard dying men talk before. Throw out your gun and I'll get you back to town for Doc to patch you up."

The laugh was eerie and high pitched. "Sure, patch me up so you can have me hanged? No chance, detective. You come in and dig me out."

Spur wished he had brought a few sticks of dynamite. He would remember to carry some next time. Spur judged the condition of the man. He could pull a trigger, but how were his reflexes? Spur had to know. He eased to a standing position, broke open the shotgun, popped out the spent shells, and pushed two new ones in.

"I can wait as long as you can, killer," Spur said.

Another round came from the gun inside the cave, and the instant it exploded, Spur took three long steps across the front of the cave, dove and rolled the remaining half dozen feet and was on the far side of the opening where the girls stood against the bluff wall.

Abby stared at him in disbelief and started to cry, but he held up a hand to stop her. He heard soft swearing from the cave mouth. Gently Spur pushed the tied-on six-gun muzzle away from Abby's chin, then cut the strings that held it in place.

"Spur!" Abby screamed. "He's pulling the string tied to the other pistol!"

Spur looked at Kitten standing tall and naked with the pistol barrel tied to her chest and now touching her chin. He saw the string tighten as the killer tugged the line from the shadows.

"No! Damnit, no!" Spur bellowed and charged toward the deadly weapon.

CHAPTER 14

SPUR RUSHED THREE STEPS to the naked girl, grabbed the six-gun's cylinder so it couldn't turn and breathed easier. With other hand he drew a knife from the inside of his boot and sliced the cords that held the pistol in place, then cut the rope that held the girl's feet to the stake driven into the ground.

A pair of shots sounded in the cave, close to the front. Spur ducked and pulled the women down as singing lead whispered over their heads. He took off his light jacket and gave it to Abby who was shivering.

"We'll get your clothes back soon," Spur said, wishing again that he had brought some dynamite with him. One stick thrown into the cave would disable a man long enough for Spur to rush in and capture him. Now he had to do it the hard way.

In the flickering light of the burning log, McCoy checked the loads in both the captured six-guns. He cocked the weapons and looked into the blackness of the cave. Spur didn't know what was inside, or where the bushwhacker was, but he had to go in. He would do it with firepower. He swung up the shotgun and blasted one double-ought buck round into the cave, then charged into the blackness. He pushed the shotgun back in his belt, fisted one of the pistols in each hand, and ran, firing a shot with every other step, dodging from side to side, looking for a muzzle flash ahead. He knew he would be outlined by the light of the fire for a few dangerous seconds, then he would be clear.

He fired six rounds and was not touched, nor did he see any sign of a gunshot ahead of him. When he was inside, he stopped firing and worked his way to one wall. The rock was cold, dry. He let his eyes adjust to the light but it was simply too dark. It was like a mile deep coal mine at midnight.

Spur stopped breathing and listened. A sound came, a shuffling, as if one boot was being dragged over the rocks. The hunter was hit, now he was the prey. Spur moved into the cave, holding one hand in front of him, stepping carefully. He stopped again and listened. The shuffling had ceased. McCoy reached in his pocket for the round pack of pasted together paper matches, ripped off two of the "stinkers" by feel and scratched them on the rough base. They flared into light, blazed up for a moment and Spur saw that the cave was ten feet high and twice that wide. He let the matches burn down to his fingers and dropped them, then turned and went back to the friendly sight of the glowing light of the fire.

He lit two more matches near the front of the cave and found the women's clothing. When Spur carried the clothes outside, he saw that Abby had built up the fire with some sticks and a pair of gnarled, pitch filled knots.

Abby took Kitten's clothes, talked to her softly, and helped her dress.

Spur let the knots burn and when one was about half ablaze, he picked it up.

"Going in and find that Jasper and settle my account. He owes me. He also owes both of you. He'll pay."

Abby nodded. She pulled on her clothes and watched him leave, then put her arm around Kitten and the two huddled close to the growing fire.

Spur moved quickly with the torch across the first fifty feet. Then he slowed, seeing that the tunnel was narrowing, the ceiling barely high enough to walk without stooping.

He moved more cautiously now, holding the torch away from him, glad that the pitch kept the flames alive and lighting the way, but knowing he made a perfect target. His hope now was that the killer ahead of him was wounded so badly that he couldn't use his weapon.

The roof slanted down sharply, and Spur had to bend over and move slower. He swung the torch from side to side. The cave had narrowed as well and was little more than six feet wide. Something moved ahead and he leveled one of the pistols at it. Spur walked closer and something moved again, on the ground. The rattle came through clear. A rattlesnake!

He shoved the torch at the viper, watched the snake strike at the flames and writhe in pain as the burning pitch stuck to the fangs and mouth. Spur's heavy boot smashed the wriggling snake's head as it fought against the burning pitch.

Spur moved forward slowly.

A revolver shot echoed loudly from ahead but no bullet came toward Spur. He moved again. Spur could still walk by bending over in the tunnel.

Without the torch he would have fallen into it.

A trench across the tunnel floor gaped suddenly directly ahead of him. There appeared to be no far side of the level on which Spur stood. He swung the torch downward and saw movement. Something slithered past him and went over the edge, dropping ten feet to the floor of the hole.

Another six-gun shot sounded and Spur jerked his head around to look at the far end of the hole. He held the torch so that it made out the form of a man lying on the bottom of the pit.

Dozens of long slender sticks covered him, but the sticks moved and rattled and struck at the man again and again.

Spur closed his eyes for a moment. No one should die that way. The bushwhacker must have been struck a hundred times by snakes from the massive ball of rattlers. The three rounds he had left in his .44 wouldn't help much. Spur shook his head and turned, sidestepping a thick, six-foot long rattler that slithered past, ignoring him. The snake fell into the pit. That kind of a dark, all-alone, rattlesnake end was a tough way for any man to die.

Two hours later, Spur dropped off the black a block from the hotel, and let the women ride on into town to the Drover's Cottage. The Sheriff was at the doctor's office getting patched up. Spur walked quickly, went in the back door and up the side stairs and inside Abby's room as Abby and Kitten arrived.

The young girl had bounced back to her usual bright, uninhibited self. But to Spur it all seemed a little forced. He talked with Abby quietly in one corner of the room after they insisted that Kitten take a nap. She hadn't slept at all the previous night.

It was just daylight when they had come into town, and now the sun was climbing. It was going to be a boiling hot day.

Abby kissed Spur softly on the lips and blinked tears back. "I'll try not to get all gooey and emotional, but I thank you for saving my life."

"I was the reason you got in the situation, I owed you at least that much."

"I'll show you my gratitude later."

"Did he rape her?"

"No, he said he would wait for both of us until he killed you. He was confident. He'd done this before. He bragged."

"He won't ever do it again." Spur told her quietly what had happened to the bushwhacker.

"Horrible!"

"He paid for his crimes. He paid all at once when he fell into that pit and realized where he was. He suffered ten minutes of pure hell."

Spur looked over and saw Kitten sleeping. Now she looked thirteen.

"You better get some sleep too," he told Abby.

"I'd rather go up to your room and thank you properly."

"Then we sleep?"

"Once is never enough."

"Leave a note for Kitten in case she wakes."

Spur's room was on the shady side of the building. They pulled the blinds and Spur began to undress her slowly, kissing away each garment. She stopped him.

"No, no! Hurry. Right now. Don't even take off your pants. Just open them and push up my skirt. Darling, I want you inside me this very second!"

Spur poised over her for a moment and then thrust into her heartland, into the crevice that was warm and wanting, waiting and wonderfully wanton.

"Don't move," she whispered. Her arms locked around his shoulders and she pulled his weight down on her as they pushed deeper into the soft mattress and Abby sighed.

"Oh, yes! If this isn't heaven, I don't know how heaven could be any better."

"Do you want to go to sleep now?"

She shook her head, and he saw tears at the corners of her eyes. He kissed them away. She cried softly. Spur let her cry. He held her head, lay his face beside hers and kissed her cheek. After three or four minutes she swallowed down the last sob and pushed his face away so she could see him better.

"I want to explain. It isn't the sex. I've made love before and I've . . . you know . . . done all that. But I've never met anyone like you. You saved my life today. I . . . just . . . don't . . . know . . . what . . . to . . .

do. I know it's not ladylike or polite or that it is just never, never done. But I can't help it. I want to take you home with me and marry you and settle down and raise your babies." She stared at him, then pulled his face down and kissed him. Her body hadn't moved since she began talking. She blinked back another spate of tears.

"Now, you can laugh at me or spank me, or roll me out of your bed, but I've had my say. I know you're not the marrying kind—I've known that from the very first moment I saw you on the train just out of St. Louis. But I've had my say and I mean every word of it."

She smiled, smudged away drying tears and her hips began a playful little motion that developed into a grinding rhythm that set Spur's teeth chattering.

He remembered what she had said. Abby would make an outstanding wife for any man, but she was right. He wasn't ready for marriage, not for a long time. He knew he was passing up a treasure. But then the full impact of what she meant hit him and he thrust into her deeper and harder. She worked her magic muscles again and he wanted to purr. A sense of desire and love surged over him. Spur knew he loved this marvelous woman.

She responded and moaned softly with delight as her hips continued to move. Her legs came around his back and worked up higher until he rested them on his shoulders and she was mewing and moaning in pleasure with little yelps of passion fulfilled.

He caught her soft buttocks and lifted her off the mattress, impaling her deeper than ever before until she squealed and moaned again, panting now, then rumbling and going off like a string of firecrackers as a long swift, violent series of spasms racked her tender body and set her face into a withing mass of erotic pleasure.

"Oh, god, Spur, marvelous, wonderful!" Then she couldn't talk, only feel and respond and let her body float away into total physical and emotional ectstacy.

Before she had finished Spur felt his own climax coming.

He shouted a hoarse bellow and rose to his knees, hoisting her with him as he pumped at her again and again and again.

The whole room exploded with fire and stars, sunsets and sweet smelling flowers and soft woodlands and mountain peaks tipped with glistening snow. Then the scene shifted away and blurred and faded into a dazling white that melted into reality. Spur let her down and lay full length beside her, arms wrapped around her protectingly and they both drifted softly to sleep.

Spur came awake three hours later. He felt strangely at peace, though drained, exhausted and still tired from his sleepless night, but ready to take on the battle again. He was lying beside Abby, he could feel her pressed against him, but curiously he felt something at his other side as well. Cautiously he opened his eyes and turned his head slightly.

Beside him as naked as he was lay Kitten, sleeping soundly. Spur knew he had locked the door. But he had left the key in the simple lock, turned half way so no one could use another key or jimmy the simple lock open. Someone had.

He tried to lift off the bed without waking either naked girl, but managed to rouse them both. He stood, pulled on his clothes smoothly. Abby and Kitten watched him.

"I like to see a man dress," Kitten said. "It's so different from a girl."

"Not when you wear pants and a shirt," Spur said. He turned to Abby who sat up, naked yet perfectly at ease in what should have been an embarrassing situation.

"Abby, there's one source left in town we haven't tapped. That newspaper man, what was his name?"

"Thaddeus, Thaddeus Obert. Strange name. He's only been in town about three months. Nobody is sure where he came from or where he got the money for the small newspaper. Everyone seems to think that he's losing money on it."

Spur watched her with amazement. "You do good research. I should keep you around."

"Don't threaten me!" she jibed, then grinned. "I do like you, though."

Kitten giggled. "You sure do! You two were just fucking up a storm when I came in. You didn't even hear me. You were good together."

Abby turned, her face blushing.

"Abby, it's all right," Kitten said. "I watched all the time at the saloon. The girls said it was the only way I'd learn how to please a man. You sure know how. Jesus!"

"Don't use profanity, Kitten," Abby said turning back, composed. "That part of your life is all over."

"True," Spur said looking at Kitten's budding figure. "Now both of you get some clothes on. Abby, you have to come with me and we'll make that newspaperman tell us everything he knows."

Twenty minutes later a decorously dressed Abby walked into the small newspaper office. No one was there. Abby pushed a little bell on the counter and a moment later a man backed out of swinging doors, a printer's composing stick in his left hand. A half line of type was set in the stick.

"Morning. This is Wednesday, press day, so I'm a little busy. What can I do for you?"

"I'm new in town and want to subscribe to your paper and take out a small advertisement."

He brightened, put down the type stick and smiled.

"Yes, always have time for business. Here is a subscription form, just fill out your name and address and we'll deliver you a paper every Thursday morning."

She picked up a pen. "I was thinking about a quarter of a page advertisement, how much would that be?"

Thaddeus glowed. She imagined he didn't sell a quarter page ad more than once a month. He took out a small card and looked down a column.

"Let's see, quarter page. Run it once or weekly?"

"Weekly for a while. Oh dear!" She gasped and caught at her throat. "Oh!"

"What's the matter?" he asked, concern lining his face.

"Feel faint, where can I sit down, lie down? Don't want to fall."

He rushed around the small counter and caught her arm. "Right back here, there's a cot. Can you walk?" She nodded. He helped her through the curtain into a back room where the smell of newsprint and wet ink enveloped them. He led her to a cot a dozen feet ahead and she sat down heavily. He knelt in front of her.

Abby pressed fingers to her head. "Feel like I'm strangling. Let me open these tight buttons." She undid three of the fasteners up to her chin and took deep breaths. She could see him watching her breasts as she exaggerated her breathing.

"Oh, it's so warm in here." She opened two more buttons on her dress top so her clevage showed. He looked down then up at her.

"Is that better, could I get you some water?"

"Yes, that would help."

He got up, hurried away and returned with a cup of water. She had unfastened another button so more of the tops of her breasts showed. She had left off her camisole and binder so her breasts strained to burst from the tight dress. He knelt in front of her and gave her the water. She drank it, then bent forward holding her head. The movement would let her breasts swing free and he could look down the open front of her dress. She allowed him a good look, then leaned back. She knew that Spur must be watching from the curtained doorway.

"Oh, thank you, I'm feeling better now." She smiled. "Thaddeus, you seemed interested in my breasts. Oh, I don't mind. Would you like a better look? It's fine with me."

He knelt in front of her. For a moment he didn't respond, then he nodded. She caught one of his hands and pushed it down the front of her dress and left it curved around a bare breast as she undid the rest of the buttons and shrugged the dress off her shoulders letting it fall to her waist. Her big breasts billowed out, swaying gently, their nipples firm, risen, turning a deep red now that they were exposed.

"Jeeze, beautiful," he said. He reached up and touched them again and Abby shivered. She saw Spur come through the doorway, a scowl building into fury on his face.

"You! Printer!" he bellowed. Thaddeus pulled back his hands and jumped up, terror etched his face.

Spur's right hand twitched over his holstered six-gun.

"Draw, you rapist! I'm gonna shoot your balls off and then slice up your dick for rat food!"

"No, no, it isn't that. The lady was faint, we just came back here to . . ."

"I *see* what you're doing, rapist. You better draw, get that hide out so you can die like a man with a gun in your fist."

"No, no! I just gave her a place to sit down and some water to drink."

"And she was so kind she let you feel her bare tits? That's my *wife* you're playing with, Buster! And that's showdown time in my book. Now, you gonna draw or do I get to do it slow and easy, one of your balls at a time?"

"I'm no gunfighter."

"Then leave my woman alone. Too fucking late for that now. Woman, get yourself covered and get back to the front office, you don't have to watch this butchering."

Abby pulled her dress up and buttoned it, patted her hair and hurried out of the print shop.

Spur drew his Merwin & Hurlburt .44 and cocked the hammer which made a deadly ominous click. "You ready to die, rapist? What was your name . . . Obert. You ready to die, Obert?"

He shook his head. "I tell you it wasn't like that at all. She was faint, and I let her sit down. Then she said she felt hot and opened some buttons. I got her a drink of water and sure I looked at them . . . beautiful breasts. Then she *asked* me if I wanted to see them. Honest to God!"

Spur brought the pistol up and aimed it at Obert's head.

CHAPTER 15

SPUR STARED AT THE trembling publisher standing beside the cot in the printer's shop.

"Bullshit! I have to coax her for half an hour to get *my* hands on her tits. You want me to think she just stripped down for you? Bullshit! You're dead, no way around it. You might as well tell me what really happened. Get it off your conscience."

"Nothing happened." Thaddeus was shaking. Spur pushed him down on the cot and towered over him. "I could stomp you back here, make less noise. Smash in your skull with my boots." Spur kicked him in the shins. "Fondle my wife's tits will you, rapist!"

Thaddeus cowered on the cot. He stared at Spur again, closer now. "Your name is Spur, right? Right. I know something about you that maybe . . . I mean it won't do you any good to kill me, a little satisfaction maybe."

Spur put the .44 against Thaddeus's forehead.

"What the hell you mean you *know* something about me? Everybody knows I'm in town working on the trail herd crew massacre."

"No, not just that. Something important. Something that could save your life, maybe even help you solve the murders."

"Sassafras juice! How'n hell could you know that?"

"How? What does that matter? *If* I know how to save your life, could we forget all about the little . . . ah, problem here? I didn't harm her, just touched her, and she asked me to. It wasn't even my fault. I never asked." He was pleading now, and inwardly Spur was grinning. "Look, I *know* I can save your life, and I *know* I can give you the facts to help you hang the key men behind this whole murder operation. I found out and I was about ready to blow apart the whole thing. They tried to kill me to shut me up, but I had sent a complete report to a friend and told him to hold it for me. If I died he was to take it to the Governor."

Spur pulled the cold steel away from Thaddeus' forehead.

"Talk."

"You've heard of the Big Four? Guess who the fourth one is. Me."

Spur laughed. "Now that will take a lot of convincing. You'll have to name names and give me dates and places, and tell me who the other Big Four are and what each does. You got some talking to do."

Thaddeus talked. Spur made him bring paper and pencil and he took notes. A half hour later Spur told him he had enough.

"That documentation you said you wrote down. Where is the copy you kept here?"

"Hidden."

"Where?"

"Under the baseplate of the small job press."

"Good, leave it there." Spur stared at him. "You know your hands are just as bloody as the riders who gun down those herd crews."

Thaddeus shrugged. "It was either that or be dead. I chose the alternative."

"You could have jumped on the train."

"True, but I didn't want to start over again without a cent."

"You testify against the other three and I can get you out of this with a reduced sentence, maybe free and clear. You have to cooperate."

"I will. I'm a newspaperman, not a conspirator. I make a hell of a lousy outlaw."

"True," Spur said. He holstered the .44.

Thaddeus scowled. "I was suckered, wasn't I? You never would have used that gun. And that woman isn't your wife is she?" He sighed. "You caught me at the right time. I really *want* out of this trap I caught myself in."

"With any luck you'll be out of it within a week," Spur said, went past the curtain and found Abby.

An hour later Spur McCoy had packed a bedroll, his change of jeans, three work shirts and a sack of grub to last him three days. After that he would eat off the trail herds. It was a little after midday when he rode south. His belly was full, and his mind churned over everything that Thaddeus had told him in his confession. From what the newsman said, the Big Four had bonded together when they couldn't get enough concessions from Joe McCoy for control of the town. They knew the only reason the trail herds came to Abilene was because it was the only spot on the rail line with pens, loading chutes, and sidings.

They intended to discourage drives from coming to Abilene. Already they were working on a new "cattle drive town" down the rail line about twenty miles. The Big Four would own the town, they would divide up the gambling halls and whorehouses, and hotels, stores and own every house and building that went up. It would be a town designed for temporary use. When the cattle drives were over in ten or twelve years, the town would die and the Big Four would all be millionaires.

But first they had to kill Abilene.

Spur rode steadily south, over the meandering swells of the prairie, moving along the natural trail that had been carved out by over a hundred thousand cattle hooves. He met one herd coming in three miles out. There were well over five thousand bawling, bellowing, dusty longhorns in the batch. Spur didn't even talk to the trail boss. No chance that he pinto pony Mex and Ben could be pushing that batch. He did check for a pinto pony among the crewmen. Failing to spot one he moved on. He passed another herd about ten miles out just before dusk. The cattle had been circled into a night herd, and the night hawks were out. He estimated that there were about two thousand beef in the lot. The trail boss was short, stocky and Polish. His name was Stanley and he was definitely in charge. Spur decided it wasn't the right crew and moved on.

He bedded down along a little creek below two giant cottonwoods, made himself a cup of coffee, and munched on some cookies that Abby had pushed into his sack of supplies. He'd been eating too much lately anyway.

Spur let his small cookfire die down, took a precautionary walk in a quarter mile circle around his camp, but found nothing unusual. By the time he got back the fire was out and he felt safe. When he rolled up in the blankets, he left his boots on and his clothes, and nestled his six-gun beside his right hand.

The next morning he rode early, found a herd three miles south, arriving in time for breakfast. The trail boss was named Yancy, Will Yancy, and he tried to hire Spur. He'd lost a crewman with a broken leg three days ago and was short-handed.

Spur told him he couldn't, briefed him about the crew murders that had taken place, and warned the man to be watchful.

"They like herds of 2,000 to 3,000," Spur said. "Be careful."

Spur took a half dozen biscuits the cook had just made on the little fold-up reflector oven, and moved down the trail.

He rode all day, meeting two more herds, both too large to be targets of the killers. From what Thaddeus told Spur, the herd had already been established for the next hit. It would be three thousand head hit two days out. He even knew the name of the outfit, the Lazy L from around Brownsville in

Texas. The chuck wagon was an older style with a large blue canvas patch on the white top. Spur ate his noon meal with one herd crew and supper with another, warning both of the danger and suggesting they double their night-hawks.

Neither of the outfits had Lazy L cattle. At least he wasn't too late. He would ride hard the next day.

Spur located the herd four days and forty miles from town. There were no different spots to get past from there on in. Everyone relaxed a little. The men were anxious to get to Abilene.

"Hey, that town as wide open as I hear? Fancy women just hanging out the windows inviting you to come on upstairs?"

Spur laughed. "That about describes it. I'm sure you'll find any kind of establishment and gambling you want in Abilene. That is if any of you make it that far."

Spur had briefed the trail boss earlier, now he was talking to the men. He gave them the whole story, about the mass grave, all the inside information he had.

"I've got permission to ride along as a spare hand. I won't help much during the day because I'll be up all night. But we want to make everything look normal. As soon as it gets dark, we'll put on extra night-hawks and keep everybody awake but in their sacks. And we'll have dummies in most of those blankets around the fire. They could hit us any time after dark, but it's my guess they wait until everyone is thoroughly asleep, and the night-hawks are getting tired too. After midnight sometime. But we have to be alert all the time. This time they might even hit us during the day."

Spur had come prepared. He showed them the cut-off shotgun and what the 12 .38 caliber slugs would do to a cardboard box at fifteen feet. The hot lead tore the box into shreds.

He had the Spencer 7-shot carbine with its .56 bore and two .44's. He talked again with the drive boss, a big hairy Irishman with a full beard, a face like a fuzzy peach and tiny black eyes that bored right through a person. His name was Jim Leslie and he had driven a herd up the previous year to Abilene.

"This bunch of cutthroats is sighting in on us?"

"That's our inside information. The two outfits ahead of you by a day are too large, 5,000 in one and nearly 6,000 in the other. The other two bunches are too close and the killers haven't hit them yet. That blue patch on your chuck wagon is a flag they can't miss."

"So be it. We'll be ready for them."

"Tonight we'll need your normal night-hawks, but I suggest half of the men be awake at all times. Put two near the fire, and dummies in the blankets. We'll spot the men around in a military type perimeter defense. I'd guess they will try for the main part of the crew first, then go for the night-hawks."

"But not tonight?" Leslie asked.

"Nobody knows. We're four days out. I'd say they'll wait until two or three days so they won't have so much trail work to do. They're rich men, they will tend to get careless, maybe even sloppy. Any of your men good with a pistol?"

"Three of them can hit something. The rest just make a lot of noise. Two don't even have guns."

"You've got nine men, including yourself?"

"Yes."

"Two night-hawks, two at the fire and the chuck wagon. One inside, one of the shooters with a rifle and two pistols. Put the other two shooters one on each side of the fire. Tell the night-hawks to take care of themselves. The killers will use knives I'd guess out there because it's quieter."

Darkness came suddenly. They built up the fire to ward off the Kansas night chill. Eight of them sat around the fire until eight o'clock, as they usually did. Now and then the men drifted off to relieve themselves. Some came back, others left. They created enough confusion so that anyone watching would have a hard time remembering who was where. Three blankets had been stuffed with brush and supplies. Two men stretched out, but kept pistols close at hand.

Spur walked the rounds talking quietly to the men. He made a deeper circle but found nothing. He kept up his patrol until midnight, then slid in for a cup of coffee they had left warming on the remains of the hot coals. He soon was back at patrol. Although he didn't expect trouble that night, they were ready. He carried two pistols, the sawed-off shotgun and the Sharps carbine.

At four A.M. Spur made one last circuit. It was too late for a strike by the killers. They would have to clean up camp, dig a hole to bury the bodies and get it all done before daylight.

At five o'clock he came in and helped the cook with breakfast. One of the wranglers had kicked up a lot of rabbits the day before. The cook skinned them out just after sundown and they had eaten most of them for yesterday's supper. They had leftover rabbit stew for breakfast. Spur figured they were short on rations and were eating off the land as much as they could.

Spur rode with the chuck wagon. It took a little over an hour to reach the noon lunch rest spot and Spur rolled out his blankets and slept for three hours.

He was good for the rest of the afternoon and night. He helped with the drag men, the three riders behind the long line of steers, calves and cows pushing them along, rounding up strays that left the line of march and generally acting as tail end Charlie. It was the toughest, dirtiest and least popular job on the drive. The men rotated from point to swing then flankers along the rear side and to drag. One man was wrangler driving their remuda of horses along with the cattle.

Once daylight came Spur felt at ease but only until dark. He felt there would be trouble. It would be tonight.

Spur left the drag team, rode north and found the trail boss three miles ahead of the herd. They talked about the chances of being attacked that night and Spur suggested they find a spot as easy as possible to defend. They had three more miles to search for an ideal place. Spur doubted they would find one, but any spot would be better than the wide open, flat plains.

They decided the best spot lay within the range of the cattle. It meant a stop a mile early, but Leslie gave his approval. There was a twenty-foot sandstone cliff to one side of a shallow valley, and a flowing stream twenty feet wide in front of it. There was room enough in the swatch of green grass in the valley for the herd to bed down. It was a logical place to spend the night. They could put the chuck wagon and campfire at the base of the cliff so they would have their backs defended. The river was four hundred yards from the cliff. The water was deep enough that a horse would have to swim to get across. That was the second natural barrier. And on the left hand side there was a Kansas thornberry thicket that not even a goat could eat its way through. That left only one side for the cutthroats to approach without some kind of problem. Good! Now, if tonight was really the night, if this was the herd they intended attacking and if they hadn't decided to end a good thing and fade away with their gold, Spur's team had a chance. There were always a lot of "if's."

Spur slept from supper to nine o'clock when Leslie woke him. The men were positioned as Spur had suggested. Four had been in the army and knew what to expect. Spur rode around the herd as a precaution. The beef were bedded down, resting. There were no storm clouds out eliminating the chance of a lightning strike. He put his horse in the rope corral and checked his weapons. The Sharps was clean and well oiled. The .44's both working perfectly. The shotgun was the simplest of the four. Spur had chosen his command post, a slight rise to the open side of the square, the side where the enemy probably would approach. He was sure if they were going to hit that night, they had been watching the herd and men most of the day. Leslie who had been a marksman with the Rebs was fifty yards beyond Spur in a line with the edge of the herd. If they came, Leslie and Jim had decided to let them sneak inside the perimeter, then open up on them from both sides.

They waited.

The camp looked normal. One or two men stirring around the fire before going to sleep. The night-hawks circled the herd, talking to the longhorns, one man whistling a home-made tune.

Spur checked the big dipper to find its movement around the north star. Its position told him it was almost ten o'clock. The killers would come within an hour.

Spur knew.

He made a silent sweep through the weeds and scrub along the edge of the river, watched and waited and listened. He heard nothing out of the ordinary.

Back at the post, lying behind an ancient two-foot cottonwood log, Spur tried to sharpen his sense of sight and hearing. He strained, concentrating on the usual sounds he might hear and tried screening them out.

Unusual, anything unusual, or out of place?

A coyote howled.

Spur scowled. He hadn't heard a coyote on this particular trip. Why now? A second coyote answered and then all was still. The calls were signals. Spur watched toward the open side of their camp.

A black blur seemed to move. McCoy concentrated on the spot. It moved again.

They were coming.

Spur watched a man working forward in the faint moonlight. Soon he picked out another man, moving silently toward them. They were five yards apart, slipping from brush to tree to rise.

In all he counted four men. That left one as back-up and one for the night-hawks.

He sighted in on the closest one, who would pass not twenty feet from where Spur lay. He couldn't shoot yet. Spur would use the Sharps. He'd let them get ten yards past him before he opened fire. Leslie must have seen them too. The firing would alert everyone.

Of the four, the man second in line seemed to be directing. The leader paused and looked at the campfire, which still blazed up now and again. Then he waved his hand forward, and the signal was passed along. Another five yards. Spur sighted in on the leader and waited.

Two more steps. They were fifteen yards inside the perimeter. Spur aimed again and was about ready to fire when Leslie's rifle cracked. Spur pulled the trigger as a reflex, and saw the man crumble and lay still. He moved his sights to the man closest to him who turned and fired a pistol. Spur fired just below the flash and heard a scream. Leslie's weapon barked twice more.

Two shots jolted into the air from the direction of the herd.

"Let's go see who we got down there," Leslie

called.

Spur rose from behind his log and stared into the muzzle of a pistol not four feet from his chest. The surprised man evidently had been moving up with the others, but was so close Spur had failed to see him.

Spur jerked his Sharps upward to fire and watched the cylinder of the revolver turn as the murdering outlaw in front of him pulled the trigger.

CHAPTER 16

SPUR INSTINCTIVELY KNEW he didn't have enough time to trigger off a shot. He continued the upward stroke with the Spencer carbine, slashing at the gun hand. Watching as in slowed down motion the Spencer's round barrel slashed toward the pistol. It seemed that time stood still while the weapons functioned. Spur lunged forward as if he held a bayonet. The arc of the Spencer barrel's path slammed steel against steel just as the six-gun's hammer fell and the black powder exploded, ramming the .44 caliber bullet out the muzzle, twisting it for a smoother flight.

Spur felt the rifle barrel strike the other weapon and bounce back and as it did he pulled the trigger. The firing almost tore the weapon from Spur's hand, but his eyes stared ahead and he saw the killer jolt backwards and drop his pistol, clutching his chest. Spur recovered his balance and stood over the fallen cowboy who grabbed for his pistol. Spur drove his boot heel down on the back of the man's hand, crushing a dozen bones and bringing a scream of pain. Spur wanted to use one more round on the killer and save a trial, but he knelt beside the man and looked at his wound. It was over his heart, perhaps through the top of his lung, but certainly not fatal.

Spur grabbed him by the arm.

"Get up you murdering bastard, you've shot your last man."

Spur pushed him ahead toward Leslie. The trail boss also had a prisoner.

"The other three are dead," Leslie said. "Where did that one come from?"

"We were using the same log, only different sides," Spur said and they pushed their captives toward the built-up fire at the chuck wagon.

A half hour later everyone on the trail drive crew was accounted for. One man suffered a minor knife wound, but he retaliated by shooting a small Mexican attacker in the face, killing him instantly.

They had four corpses and two live ones.

"Are there any more of you?" Leslie demanded from the man he captured. The cowboy didn't answer. Leslie slammed his big fist into the man's face knocking him down. When he asked the question the second time the raider said there were only six of them.

"How many crews have you killed?" Spur asked.

The outlaw was on his knees now. He looked no more than twenty years old. He shrugged. Leslie kicked him on the side of the head, a glancing blow, but it slammed the youth into the dust. He lay there not moving.

"How many crew have you killed this summer?" Spur asked again.

The young man sat up, stared straight ahead before answering slowly, "Six, maybe seven, I can't remember."

A pistol shot exploded into the silence of the Kansas night. The round tore into the cowboy's right leg and he pitched forward, holding the leg, writhing in pain, screaming in protest.

Leslie looked at Jim over the smoking muzzle of his .44.

"I say we swing the bastard to the nearest cottonwood tree right now!"

"No," Spur said softly. "We can't do that. We have no authority, no proof, no trial, no judge."

"You're talking like a lawman. Who the hell are you?"

"I'm smart enough to know that if we hang this one that makes us no better than he is." Spur looked around at the sullen faces of the eight other trail crewmen. They all were angry. They had been targeted for death. Only Spur's arrival had saved them from eternity.

"Sure, you men were the intended victims, but killing these two won't help solve the problem. Who do you suppose set up this game? Who paid these men? Who bought the cattle and split the profits? The men I want are in Abilene. The real blood suckers are those in Abilene who hired these killers."

"Then you are a lawman. Let's see your badge."

"Leslie, I'm not a sheriff or marshall or even a Pinkerton. It's my job to bring these two in alive to stand trial and make them testify against whoever hired them and set up this blood-money scheme. These six murdered at least sixty men! That demands more justice than a quick .44 slug or the end of a hemp rope out here on the prairie with no witnesses."

Leslie still held the .44. He looked at his men. "What in hell do you guys think? Your lives were on the line tonight."

"If we kill them, the big shots in town will just hire some more, Jim," one man said. "Hail, why not clean out the whole nest of snakes at once?"

"Been enough killing here tonight," another man said.

"Whatever you say, Jim."

"Hell, let's put them on horses and take all six into town tomorrow," another decided. "I'll go along and help!"

Jim Leslie shrugged. "Yeah, damnit, I guess you're right. Hell, McCoy, you can have all six. No sense letting them corpses rot for four days. We'll find their horses come daylight and tie the bodies across their saddles and you and one man can take them into town. If you start early you should get there by sundown."

Spur asked the cook to put on a pot of coffee, then he took a stub pencil from his pocket and folded a piece of paper from his jacket and talked with the shot-up outlaws. He tied up the wounds the two survivors had and then bound their ankles together. Neither man was going to run off anywhere.

Spur talked to the two killers separately. He wrote down the names of all six men in the band, their approximate ages and where they came from. Ben Hood identified himself as the leader.

Spur drew from each man accounts of the method of operation, exactly how and when they attacked each camp. He found out that a courier came out from town every two weeks to set up another herd. The courier was the newsman, Thaddeus Obert.

Spur pushed gently as he probed to find out if the men knew the names of any of the ringleaders in Abilene. They named the Big Three. They also said that the crew of six men got a one-fifth share in the profits. If they sold 2,000 held for $35 a head, that was $70,000 they split five ways into $14,000. The six men split that six ways to about $2,300. Their share of the money was all in the bank in Abilene. One man bragged that he had made over $16,000.

"You might have a credit in the bank of that much, but you'll never live to spend a penny of it," Spur said softly.

At five o'clock the following evening, Spur McCoy and his little caravan plodded into Abilene and created a sensation. It had taken them longer than expected. The horses, tied in a long pack train, had been skitterish of the dead bodies draped over them. But at last they settled down to a steady walk. The forty miles had slithered past slowly. Jim Leslie had sent along one of his wranglers to help with the pack train and to take his turn leading. They stopped at two in the afternoon and ate the last of Spur's provisions.

He lined up the six horses in front of the County Sheriff's office and swung down.

Sheriff Manfred Jurgens stepped off the boardwalk to meet Spur. He had a bandage on his left shoulder but moved easily. He had heard that dead men were coming to town.

Spur had warned the cowhand not to mention to anyone the corpses or the two live ones. Spur sent word for the town's only doctor to come to the jail. He untied the wounded men from their saddles and walked them into jail cells.

Then he told the sheriff what happened on the trail.

"And I've got enough evidence to string up three of the town's most prominent citizens. The ring-leaders of this mass murder scheme."

Spur named them, the sheriff nodded and they took two deputies and marched down the street. The doctor met them at the door. The sheriff grimly told him to patch up the two prisoners and charge it to the county.

Outside, Spur and Sheriff Jurgens walked into the nearest business of the Big Four, the Gundarian Emporium. Gundarian stood on the top of the steps leading down from his office. He watched them a moment and his face froze.

"Mr. Gundarian, you're under arrest for the trail crew killings," Sheriff Jurgens said.

Gundarian swallowed. "Yes, I heard . . . Let me get my jacket and I'll be right down."

Spur frowned and as the man walked out of sight toward his office, Spur ran for the steps. He was too late.

A muffled sound of a pistol shot came before Spur reached the first riser. Spur and the sheriff rushed up the stairs. Dennis Gundarian lay over his desk, the back of his head blown off by a .44 round. The muzzle of the pistol was still in his mouth.

Downstairs the four men moved to the next closest suspect, the newsman, Thaddeus Obert.

The door to the newspaper office was closed and a neat sign had been tacked on the front door. "Have gone to Chicago to buy a new press. Hope to return within two weeks."

Spur noticed the date on the notice. It had been put up that morning. The morning train would give Thaddeus connections to Denver and on west. They would never see the conspirator again.

At the bank, Nance Victor stared at them with shock, surprise and disbelief.

"Surely this must be a joke. I know *nothing* of any conspiracy and I certainly have had nothing to do with anyone to plan or carry out these trail herd crew killings. My records are open. I must advise you, however that I have on a retainer the best criminal lawyer in the state. He is due in tomorrow for his regular conference. He will represent me, of course, if there are any formal charges."

Spur smiled. "Formal charges will be on hand for your lawyer, Mr. Victor, along with sworn affidavits and the testimony of two of the killers who will testify against you. I hope your lawyer is a good one, and that he isn't sensitive about seeing his client hanged."

"You'll have to come with me, Mr. Victor," the sheriff said. "We still have one jail cell unfilled."

"You are out of your mind. I will not spend a minute in that filthy jail of yours!"

For a big man Sheriff Jurgens moved quickly. Before the banker could move, the sheriff had Nance Victor by one arm, spun him around and pushed him toward the two deputies.

"Afraid you'll be spending quite a few minutes with us, Mr. Victor. Take him to his new home, boys."

Deputies walked Victor out of the bank and toward the jail. As soon as they left the bank manager closed the bank.

Hans Kurtzman and his Trail's End Hotel were next on the list. Spur saw some movement at a curtained window on the second floor. Wasn't that where Kurtzman had his office? Spur let the sheriff go in the front door while he went to the rear. Kurtzman might be the kind to run if he knew he was exposed.

Spur came around the corner of the hotel in time to see a man he thought was Kurtzman riding away down the alley. Spur ran to the back door and bolted inside. The desk clerk looked up.

"Did Kurtzman just leave by the back door?" Spur asked.

The clerk yawned. "Matter of fact, he did. Said I was to take over for a couple of days. He had to go see his sick brother in Topeka. Said that I should . . ."

Spur spun around and ran out the front door, saw a cowboy just getting off his horse and pressed a twenty dollar gold piece in his hand.

"Borrow your horse for a couple of hours?"

The cowboy looked at a month's wages in his hand and nodded.

Spur stepped into the saddle and rode. Then he realized all the firepower he had were the two .44's, one still stuffed in his belt, the other in the holster.

The roan he borrowed was fresh and spirited. He raced her at a full gallop the length of the street and searched in both directions along the cross street. Kurtzman had to come this way.

Spur saw the rear quarters of a black rounding the far end of the street two blocks down. It had to be the same black. Kurtzman was heading south.

McCoy moved his animal at an easy lope, one that ate up the ground but would not wear her out quickly. He rounded the same corner and saw the black ahead of him and a rider he guessed was Kurtzman.

The hotel man didn't know horses. He was whipping the black along at a full gallop. At that speed the quarter horse was rapidly outdistancing Spur, but the agent knew that the animal could maintain the speed for no more than half a mile. Then the mount would slow of her own need. If pushed hard she could drop over dead in her tracks.

Spur watched the rider ahead. He was going past the stockyards and around a herd of beef waiting to get into the pens. There was no doubt that he was running. Spur speeded his roan so as not to lose track of the black, then eased off again when the hotel man angled into the well-worn cattle trail south. He had nothing but three hundred miles of wilderness south into Texas ahead of him.

Spur eased off more on his mount, checked both his pistols and wished he had the shotgun. Ten minutes later he saw he was catching up with the black. The big horse was not quite half a mile ahead and wavering, slipping to one side, then overcorrecting back the other way.

There was nothing Spur could do to save the horse. He didn't care about the man, but it was a shame to ride a good horse to death.

Five minutes more and the horse and rider went down. The horse tried to get up, then screamed in a high pitched fury that Spur heard a quarter of a mile away.

Kurtzman stood up, stared at Spur for a moment, then ran into the prairie.

There was no place to hide.

Spur reached the horse, saw that it was almost dead and turned into the prairie. He sighted Kurtzman running a hundred yards ahead. He stared back at Spur. Spur drew a six-gun and rode forward. Fifty yards away, Kurtzman fired at Spur. The round came nowhere near the agent, who stopped his roan and stared. Kurtzman was red-faced, one hand on his hip and a six-gun in the other. He looked as though he had never fired a pistol before.

"Put it down, Kurtzman," Spur yelled. He rode forward.

Kurtzman fired again. This time the round came close enough for Spur to hear it go by. He ducked and pushed to the far side of his roan, he leveled the pistol across the saddle. McCoy fired once at thirty yards to scare Kurtzman. He never wavered. Spur held his fire until he was at twenty yards.

Kurtzman fired again, and the bullet clutched at Spur's shirt. The agent fired again, his sights dead center on the ringleader. The bullet plowed into Kurtzman's left shoulder and staggered him backward. He lifted his right hand and aimed at Spur. The

Secret Service Agent fired twice, so fast it sounded like one round. Both heavy slugs thundered into Kurtzman's chest. He jolted backward, his knees buckled and the gun flew from his hand. He landed on his back and rolled to one side. Spur rode to him and dismounted, but was careful to see both the hotel man's hands before he moved up close. He had no other weapon.

Kurtman's eyes fluttered. He stared upward at Spur, who knelt in the soft brown summer grass.

"Why did you run? You knew you couldn't get away."

"Heard about Gundarian. I couldn't do that. No willpower. Figured you'd do it for me." He coughed and his face distorted in agony as pain smashed through him. Then it passed and he opened his eyes. "Knew you'd do it for me, thanks, McCoy." His face broke into a smile, then it froze there and a last gush of air rushed from his lungs in a death rattle. Spur reached over and closed his eyes staring into eternity.

Two down, one ran away, and one coming up for trial. The mood of the townspeople would make short work of Victor Nance, famous lawyer or no. In fact the big time lawyer would hurt him with a jury of twelve men good and true for Abilene. Spur would put out a wanted poster on Thaddeus Obert, but the chances of every finding him were slim. Spur pushed his Merwin & Hurlburt .44 back in leather. It had been a good day's work. Now, what loose ends did he have to tidy up?

CHAPTER 17

SPUR CREATED ANOTHER small sensation when he rode back into Abilene with Kurtzman's body over the horse's back just behind the saddle. He stopped at the sheriff's office. Sheriff Jurgens waved him inside.

"Sure as hell saves the county the expense of a trial, McCoy, but now I think it's past time you told me who you are."

They went into the sheriff's private office, a six-by-six foot rough room with a scarred desk and two chairs.

Spur took a folder from his pocket that doubled for holding paper money. Inside there were a pair of tin-type pictures. He pried them apart, took out a thin, printed card, and handed it to the sheriff.

> 'To whom it may concern. This is to confirm and establish that the bearer, one Spur McCoy is an active officer in the United States Secret Service, and

is empowered by the federal government with authority in any law inforcement matter of special interest to said government especially when state lines are crossed or the crimes are not being addressed by local authorities. I put my hand to this identification on this 14th day of January, 1865. Abraham Lincoln, President of the United States."

The sheriff stared at the card for several minutes, turned it over and noticed the great seal of the United States. He turned it back, read it again, then carefully handed it to Spur.

"Tarnation! Why didn't you tell me? Mr. Lincoln! President Lincoln. You ever meet him?"

"Yes, I worked in Washington D.C. for six months about that time."

Spur put the card back between the tintypes, sealed the edges again and inserted the pictures in his wallet.

"I would have told you if I needed to, Sheriff. I figured you were honest and would help get the job done. Now, about the clean-up. The trial of Nance Victor shouldn't be hard. The two killers in there will testify against him if you can work out some kind of a lesser sentence for them. Keep some of the trail crew to testify against them. I'll give a deposition to the court tomorrow, then I'll have to be moving on. I'd suggest a court order to get back as much of the money as possible for those herds that were sold. Victor will fight that, but the court should allow it. We have the names of the outfits. They buyers in town can supply the talley of critters bought. I'll leave it up to you to see that as much of that money as possible gets into the owners' hands in Texas."

"I've already got a court order working on that problem. The judge is in town on his circuit and we should be able to get it cleared up before the Victor trial."

Spur stood and shook the sheriff's hand. "Thanks for your help, Sheriff."

The big lawman grinned. "Abraham Lincoln! The President. You don't mind if I tell my family do you?"

"Not at all."

"Oh, McCoy. I have a letter for you. Came this afternoon after those bodies arrived." He handed Spur a white envelope with his name printed on the outside.

The Secret Service agent took it and walked out the door. He leaned against the outside of the jail in the sun and saw that the Abilene undertaker had already taken Kurtzman's body away. The other four were gone too. The undertaker would have a big bill for the county.

He tore open the envelope and saw a fine feminine hand. The writing on soft pink paper ran slightly uphill.

> "Mr. McCoy. It is imperative that you contact me at once. Another aspect of your case came up and we must discuss it before you leave town. I have a feeling you might be about ready to go. Please contact me at once. I'll be in my office today until six P.M." It was signed, Virginia Dale.

The lawyer. Spur folded the paper and envelope and pushed them back in his pocket. He couldn't figure out what she was worried about. There should be no legal problems. He might have to show her his Secret Service card, but he hoped not. The more anonymous he could remain concerning his official position, the better. It was service policy and suited him as well.

He stepped off the boardwalk, walked across the dusty street, avoiding the horse droppings swarming with flies, and climbed the steps to the lawyer's office on the second floor.

He started to knock on the door to her small office, then turned the knob, pushed the panel open and walked inside.

The office was as it had been before: about ten-feet square with a fine oak desk and chair, a file cabinet and some bookshelves.

But there was no woman lawyer.

Then he saw the door open at the back of the room.

"Yes? I'll be right there."

It was the woman lawyer's voice. He waited. A moment later she came through the door. She wore a frilly dress tight at the waist and brushing the floor with a touch of a bustle and tight across modest breasts.

"Oh, Mr. McCoy." Her hands went to her hair then fluttered to her sides. "I . . . I was just closing. Would you mind if we talked in my living room? I stay in back." Her hair was not pinned but fell in a billowing black river down her back and over her shoulders. He had forgotten how tall she was.

"I wouldn't mind at all, Miss Dale. I still owe you my thanks for getting me freed after that trumped-up arrest."

The flicker of a smile touched her serious face, then

was gone only to be replaced by a slightly forced smile as she led the way into her living quarters behind her office. Many professional people lived that way in frontier towns. It reduced the cost of doing business.

The living room was tastefully arranged. The walls were papered, the woodwork painted, and an attractive spread covered what he guessed was an old sofa. Several pictures hung on the wall including one of Miss Dale in cap and gown.

She motioned for him to sit on the sofa, and she sat a respectable distance away.

"Mr. McCoy I shouldn't have sent the note. I mean . . . I have no professional reason for asking you to see me."

"Good," Spur said smiling. "I never did really thank you properly for what you did at my trial."

She frowned.

"That time I kissed you. I figure I owe you at least two more for your fine defense."

"Oh!" It was small and surprised, perhaps a little expectant.

Spur moved beside her, lifted her chin and kissed her soft lips. She closed her brown eyes, and a soft, gentle sound came from her throat as their lips parted. Spur edged closer, put his arms around her and kissed her again, holding her against him, his lips more demanding this time. It was a long kiss. When at last he eased his mouth from hers, she lay in his arms and slowly blinked open her eyes.

"Oh, my, Mr. McCoy!"

"Did you like that?"

"Oh, my, yes. Nice, it was nice and gentle."

"Then we should do it again." He bent slowly and her eyes closed, her lips parted slightly as he touched them, and his tongue brushed against her quivering mouth. She moaned in response and his tongue broke past her lips into her mouth. Darts of fire seemed to jolt into him as their tongues met, parried and twined, their juices mingling.

Suddenly she pushed back and sat away from him.

"Mr. McCoy," she said, her eyelids lowered so he could barely find her brown eyes. "I work in a man's world with lawyers and judges and all men juries. I have to be direct and forceful and sometimes I get demanding. I also deal in fact." She began unbuttoning the top of her dress.

"Mr. McCoy, I'm twenty-six years old and a virgin. I wish I wasn't. I want you to help me solve that problem." The buttons were open halfway down. "Would you mind terribly coming into my bedroom?"

Spur reached over and helped her unbutton the rest of the fasteners to her waist.

"Miss Dale, I would be honored and highly pleased to come to your bedroom." His hand slid inside the open dress front and touched one of her breasts through the soft cotton cloth covering. She gasped, pulled back, then sighed and smiled.

"Are you sure? I'm totally a beginner."

His hand pressed forward again, worked through her garment and closed around her pulsating breast. She shivered, then smiled.

"Miss Dale, at making love there are no beginners,

only some more experienced than others."

He stood, caught her hand and lifted her to her feet. She led the way again into her bedroom, which was totally feminine. The paper was pink, the bedspread pink with rows of ribbons and lace. A small dresser and chest of drawers were painted white with pink rose decorations. Pictures of family adorned the walls and a small white cat lay on the bedspread.

She moved the cat off the bed and turned, standing close to him.

"Do you want to undress me now?"

"I've wanted to undress you since the moment I saw you," Spur said. "But there's no hurry. Let things take their natural course." He sat on the bed and she sank down beside him. He kissed her again, his hand finding her right breast as their tongues twined. She sighed and whimpered in surprise when he caught her shoulders and pulled her down, she spread half on top of him.

"There's really nothing hard or complicated. Making love is the most natural act most people ever do. We'll move at the speed you want to." His hand found the key and wormed under her last inner garment so his fingers touched and then held her bare breasts.

She shivered, then stared at him, surprised.

"Why, that's delightful! I like your touch, your caressing me . . . there. Before it had been . . . I was frightened. I made him stop. Now, now it's so . . . such a natural feeling." She pushed higher on him so she could reach his lips and kissed him. He used both hands now and worked the dress off her shoulders. He turned her and lay her on her back, then began loosening and removing her dress. He kissed away the straps and chemise and at last she lay on the bed bare to the waist.

Her breasts were modest with light pink areolas and small pink nipples. He kissed her lips, then down her chin and neck and across her chest to one breast. She gasped when he kissed the orb and then licked her nipple.

Virginia Dale climaxed. Her body shook and trembled and she moaned and cried out sharply once, then melted into a delightful shivering.

"Oh, so beautiful! I've never felt anything so marvelous!"

"Miss Dale, that's only the beginning of the wonderful things you're going to be feeling today."

She sat up then and undressed him, savoring each moment, growing more and more excited as Spur's large muscular body became exposed. When at last she pulled off his pants and his underwear, she gasped in surprise.

"You mean that . . . that huge thing is going to . . ." She sat down on her bed in astonishment.

Spur lay beside her and moved her hands down to hold the object of her amazement.

"Remember we were talking about natural and easy? When it happens it will be the most natural thing in the world."

She sat up and pushed him down on his back. "I want to *look* at you. My goodness you are so large, I don't mean just him, I mean *all* of you. And so many *muscles.* Your shoulders are so wide and strong, and your flat little belly and such strong, *powerful* legs. Then, of course, there is the interesting part."

She laughed. "Honestly I can't believe this is me. I'm talking like a crazy person. It's just covering up for my surprise and my delight." She was kneeling over his side, and now moved so one breast dangled over his face. Slowly she lowered it and he kissed it, then opened his mouth and she lowered it more until he had pulled as much of her breast into his mouth as he could.

Virginia Dale moaned with delight, and a moment later moved her other orb into his mouth.

Slowly, bit by bit, he moved her along until at last she was eager to have him take her. She watched him kneel over her and her eyes were bright.

"I've heard that it hurts the first time."

"Sometimes, but just think how good it will feel."

Suddenly she closed her legs and turned away. "No, I don't want to."

He kissed her, seduced her all over again, and an hour later, their bodies joined.

She cried out in surprised delight, and kissed him wherever she could reach his body.

"Why didn't you *tell* me it was so marvelous!" she groused at him. "So amazing, so delicious! Again, I want to do it again."

He laughed and told her it would take him a few minutes to get his strength back.

"Why?" she asked.

"Boys are different from girls," he said and they both laughed, gently savoring the honest joy of the moment.

It was almost dusk when Spur dressed and walked down the wooden steps from the three offices on the second floor. It would be a long time before he forgot Virginia Dale.

CHAPTER 18

SPUR McCOY STRODE directly to the Silver Spur saloon. He looked around and spotted Lily talking with four cowboys at a table. When Spur tapped Lily on the shoulder, she grinned and grabbed him in a bear hug.

"Coo, Luv. Where'n hell you been keeping yourself?"

"Busy," he said. "We've got to talk. Upstairs?"

She smiled, winked and led him through the back curtain and up the steps.

"Wondering, Luv, when you would come see me again. I missed you, indeed I did. There is them who have it and them who don't and never will. You have it, dearie!"

Inside her apartment, she closed the door and opened her arms. Spur folded his arms and frowned at her.

An hour later they lay on the bed still wrapped in

each other's arms. Spur stroked her breasts and she purred softly.

He had collected the three thousand two hundred dollars from Lily. He would keep it in the bank and have the bank send a monthly draft to Kitten wherever she lived. It meant that the rest of her childhood would be normal. The scars of the past few months would heal quickly in one so young. Abby wanted to stay in St. Louis for a while with Kitten. She had some time off coming. It would be pleasant, an almost ready-made family for the three of them.

Soon Spur would have another assignment to pick from the stack of five or six that he was sure the Service would have ready for him. He often thought of asking for a transfer back to Washington, D.C. and the big city's bright lights. But then he would be missing all the excitement out West.

Spur reached down and kissed Abby's nipples. They trembled. He kissed them again and her eyes came open so he could see the glint there. Her hands reached for him and Spur laughed softly. Until they came to St. Louis it was going to be one exhausting trip. But there was no chance he wanted to change it, not one little bit!

"She's only thirteen."

"Who? What the hell you talking about?"

"Kitten."

"No, you can't mean Kitten. You the one who kidnapped her? Hell, she told me herself she was a week past her fifteenth birthday first thing when she got here."

"Thirteen. She won't be fourteen for two months yet. You made a whore out of her when she was thirteen. You know what the judge will do to you? You're going to get to know the inside of the territorial women's prison right well."

"Dear god, what are you talking about?"

"Kitten. You owe her just one hell of a lot, Lily. And I intend to see that you pay, one way or another. I can go to the sheriff and swear out a complaint and get a warrant, or you can do the right thing by the child and hope that she can get herself readjusted to the normal world and go on with her childhood."

"You're serious, aren't you?" Lily asked.

"Damn serious, Lily. Was business that bad?"

"No. Damn!" Lily paced the confines of her living room. She came up to him. "Spur, you know how it is. We have to put in an order for girls once a year. The ones here get used up and hurt or married and drift off. I ordered and some asshole in Chicago sent me Kitten. She said she was sixteen, but I knew she wasn't. Hell, fifteen ain't so bad. Lots of girls get married younger than that. So what the fuck. I had already paid a hundred for her and another hundred for rail fare. I knew he wouldn't give me my money back. So . . . ."

"So now you made good. Have you ever *seen* a woman's federal prison? This is interstate shipment of a minor for white slavery. That makes it federal. I can lock you in county jail within an hour. The sheriff will close up your place here and sell it to help pay your fine of about twenty-thousand dollars. The law doesn't look kindly on white slavery of underage girls."

"Or else you'll do what? What are you getting at, Spur?"

"Or else you take care of her. You ship her back to Chicago, and set up a trust fund for her in a bank paying her forty dollars a month until she's twenty-one. That's three thousand and two hundred dollars. And that's in cash. I'll give you a receipt and send a copy of the trust fund agreement to the sheriff. He'll deliver it to you. You have two days to raise the money. The bank is closed but you know the banker."

Spur stopped and stared at the painted, pretty, fancy lady. She gave a big sigh and moved closer to him, rubbing her breasts on his chest.

"Spur. I don't have that kind of money. Can't we talk this over in the bedroom? I could stand a good rough working over right now."

Spur shook his head. "Sorry, Lil, I've got two ladies waiting for me. I owe them dinner. Remember, two days. Have the cash in U.S. banknotes. It's so much easier to carry." He touched his fingers to his brow and walked away. She called but he didn't turn around. He could imagine how she had opened her dress top letting her magnificient breasts flow out to entice him. "See you in two days, Lily," he said and walked down the steps and out through the saloon to the street. He would just have time to make the dining room with his two ladies before the big rush started.

It took Spur and Abby two days to convince Kitten that she should go back to Chicago. At last she gave up, crumbled, and cried and Abby cried too.

"I've never been so scared in my life," Kitten said, tears still running down her pink cheeks. "I didn't ever know why that man bought me the ticket, not until we got here." She wiped tears away and looked up.

"Mr. McCoy, you mean I can have a nice place to stay and go to school and not have to . . . you know, make those men happy?"

"You can have the rest of your childhood, enjoy growing up, back there in Chicago somewhere. You said you have an uncle? I'll make sure he'll treat you right. Now, don't you think it's about time you started packing?"

"Pack what?" Kitten said. "This is it, just what I'm wearing."

Abby shook her head. "The stores didn't have *anything* in her size. Just wait until we get to St. Louis. We'll buy the stores out." She grinned at Spur. "You know. it's almost like. . . ." She stopped.

Spur nodded. "I know exactly what you mean. Now, I have to talk one more time with the prosecutor and the judge. Then I'm through. Looks like our banker friend Nance Victor will have a good long stay in the federal prison. The judge is due to start the trial tomorrow." Spur went to the door and looked back. Kitten was leaning into Abby's arms. The pretty railroad detective had melted and was holding her tenderly.

"You two be packed and ready to leave in two hours. The train will be here about four and we want to be ready." He watched them a minute then went into the hall.

The sheriff had moved into action fast. He had the two wounded killers patched up, in the saddle and leading him and a posse to as many of the grave sites as they could remember. They uncovered six. At the trial both men were found guilty of murder and ordered hanged. It was a short trial.

When Spur, Kitten and Abby stepped on board the train a half hour later, Spur was impressed.

Abby was bubbling and excited. "I knew this car was coming through but not quite certain when, so I found out. Isn't it gorgeous?"

Spur looked inside the door of the private railroad car. It was the last word in luxury and comfort. Almost sixty feet long, it contained two bedrooms, a living room and dining area, its own bathroom and closets. It was carpeted, with varying shades of velvet upholstery on the swiveling arm chairs with long braided fringes. Velvet tufted curtains bordered each window, and large mirrors served as panels. The ceiling was covered with scrollwork and enamel work billowing to a large gas light in the bulging top of the car. It looked more like an expensive grand ballroom entrance than a rail car.

Spur had seen the President's private rail car, but it was not a bit nicer than this one.

"I don't believe it!" Kitten yelped. "I sat up in a wooden bench when I came here from Chicago."

"You won't have to sit up going home, Kitten. Come, let's look at your bedroom."

Spur felt the train lurch and the trip had started.

Abby came back alone.

"Kitten was so thrilled with the room she decided to stay there a while," Abby said. "I had to use some favors to get permission to use this private car to St. Louis, but I knew Kitten would love it."

"And you did say there were two bedrooms."

Abby smiled. "There hasn't been much time for us since Kitten arrived. Maybe now."

Spur bent and kissed her. "I'm sure there will be lots of time. But none for cards."

"We never did get to play cards coming here, did we?"

"No."

"Spur McCoy. I want to show you our bedroom."

"Is there a lock on the door?"

Abby smiled. "Oh, yes, there sure is—and it works!"